Here a

A Collection of Short Stories

W Lodwick Lowdon

'Whether in the Outback of Australia or in an English Country Garden W. Lodwick Lowdon casts a wry and perceptive eye over the human condition providing many a surprise along the way.'

Bernard Pearson, Poet, author of *In Free Fall*.

'A fine anthology of stories, from opposite sides of the world, written by someone with experience and appreciation of both cultures.'

R. J. Turner author of *A Perfect Alibi*.

'Lodwick Lowdon seems to be bi-lingual. Her stories highlight the fact that Australians and the British speak the same language so differently. The characters stay with you long after the book has been closed.'

Vicky Turrell author of *It's Not A Boy*.

Published by Leaf by Leaf Press Ltd 2018
www.leafbyleafpress.com

Copyright © Wendy Lodwick Lowdon 2018

W Lodwick Lowdon has asserted her right to be identified as the author of this work in accordance with the Copyright, Design and Patents Act 1988

ISBN 978-0-9957154-6-2

All rights reserved. No part of this publication may be reproduced, stored in or introduced into a retrieval system, or transmitted in any form by any means without the prior written permission of the publisher. Any person who does an unauthorised act in relation to this publication may be liable to criminal prosecution and civil claim for damages.

Printed and bound in Great Britain by Clays Ltd, Elcograf S.p.A.

'I find for a moment in my mind the sound of a voice, or the sense of a motion, a gesture, a distance. These don't fit into my memories of my life here.'

City of Illusions by Ursula Le Guin.

Acknowledgements

I thank Dave, my husband, for his belief in and support for my stories. He has given me time, comment and supported my patchy computer skills. He has provided the superb photographs for this book.

I also thank members of Leaf by Leaf Press, Vicky Turrell, Ron Turner, John Heap, Bernard Pearson and Trixie Roberts, for encouraging me and helping me knock these stories into shape. I thank the members of Oswestry Writers Group for listening and urging me to keep writing.

Thank you, John and Sara Heap, for formatting and enabling the printing of this book. Thank you, Helen Baggott, for proofreading the manuscript. All remaining mistakes are my own.

Finally, I wish to acknowledge the contributions of my family, friends and a few strangers who provided the seeds for many of these stories, which I have worked to grow and prune into shapes divergent and different from their starting point.

Foreword

The stories in this collection are drawn from a life lived half in Australia and half in Great Britain. These countries share the English language but in many and unexpected ways the countries differ as did the way I lived in each.

In Australia I lived a wandering life. At first because my parents moved incessantly, I attended fourteen schools. However, when I was able to choose, I too elected to move from place to place. It gave rise to a fringe dwelling way of life so I tended to observe rather than participate but my family, and the friends that held on despite my nomadic lifestyle, have kept me anchored and happy.

Marriage took me to Great Britain and I approached moving to a different country with an insouciance derived from having moved so often in the past – how difficult was it going to be? It proved to be difficult and required more profound adjustments than I had anticipated.

In England I have lived a settled life. I have lived in the same parish and in the same house in for almost twenty-seven years. I have, perforce, engaged in the local society. Dave; his mother, Glenys; Andrew, the English son with an Australian passport; visits from my parents, siblings and cousins; a cheerful sequence of kelpies and good, local friends assisted me to stay and settle in this new, sometimes strange land.

I do think that geographically and socially I have lived two vastly different lives.

Contents

The Stockman	1
A Better Bit of Luck	6
Shoes	14
A Particularly Long Absence	20
The Haunting	27
The Old Dog	32
The New Car	37
Lightning Ridge	45
The Camping Host	53
True Believers	60
Rubbish	65
It'll Be Grand	72
Edith Williams	76
Growing At Home	85
Discretion	93
New Blood	102
The Shout	108
Changing Tunes	113
Staying Put	123

Here and There

A Collection of Short Stories

W Lodwick Lowdon

Celia,

With love,

Wendy

Here and There

The Stockman

It was mid-afternoon. The heat shimmer had eased and the gums cast long shadows. The sheep had done about seven miles already and the stockman was satisfied they could easily do two more. He reckoned they would reach the holding paddocks and borehole water before dark. He was on his own but three hundred head of sheep only need a man on a horse and a couple of dogs.

He relaxed in the saddle, confident he and the dogs would keep them straight. All he had to do was keep the mob moving; not too fast as it was the hurrying that stressed sheep and it made them more unpredictable. Just push them along slowly and let them grab a bit of grass by verges from the run-off. He whistled Bob in; he was a young dog and a bit too keen. Old Meg, now, she knew the route and she was content to trot quietly at the back of the mob. The stockman dismounted. He liked to walk his horse while he rolled a smoke. He whistled again to Bob to bring him in behind.

The campsite took him by surprise. Just a few hundred yards to the north, was a town of tents. There was a huge mushroom in the middle and an avenue of smaller fungi dotted in an arc around it. Behind the tents was a large truck, yellow and crowded with frames and drills. The stockman nodded. He'd heard that there were drillers on Casey's land; private property above ground but the government had the right to poke around underground. The stockman wasn't sure about the logistics or the legalities but there was bound to be some potential for a bit of money for Casey whatever the outcome, lucky bugger.

He couldn't see any movement. Good thing too as he'd really no time for a yarn if he was to settle the mob by dark. He remounted and pressed the horse into a trot. Maybe he'd catch up with a few of the blokes in Georgetown Pub and get a bit of news; well, only if they were talkers rather than fighters.

The stockman dragged his eyes and mind back to the drive. Another hour and he'd be able to pen the sheep. Mike would come in the morning and help him load them onto the train.

The brace of tents close to the droving route shuddered as a few of his sheep tripped over the guy ropes. The stockman sent Bob away to the left to head them off and push them away from the tents and closer to the fence that lined the track on the right. He whistled to Meg to push up the speed and she darted at the stragglers and created a wave of movement that quaked through the whole mob. Why the hell were there two tents here? They must be half a mile from the tent city.

The stockman smothered his cursing and raised his hat to the white woman in the floral cotton dress who appeared out of one of the tents. She had a kid squirming on her hip and a little girl holding onto her dress. The woman raised her hand in return before she turned to close the tent flaps against the dust lifted into the air by the passing sheep. The blue-eyed, hatless little girl let go of her mother's skirt and stepped forward to watch. He waved at her. She grinned and waved back.

More sheep jostled the tents and he signalled Bob to keep them to the left. Meg still hounded the stragglers and the pace increased even more when the stockman cracked his whip and weaved the stock horse close to the back of the mob. The tow-headed girl continued to watch, gripped by the fluid movement of man on the horse and the quick tacking of the dogs.

Most of the mob had been herded past the tents but a stubborn knot of sheep were stuck between the tents. The stockman whistled Bob. Nothing; there was no red dog nipping at the sheep. The stockman was puzzled and annoyed. He turned in his saddle and called up Meg to drive the blundering and protesting sheep back into the flock. He then had to turn his horse and ride back a hundred or so yards to gather up a couple of bolters and the whole momentum of the mob slowed.

It took several more minutes for the stockman to urge all of the sheep past the snag of tents and, though he had whistled shrill summons, without the help of Bob. The little girl pointed to a depression about sixty yards beyond the tents. The stockman rode over and found Bob scavenging in a rubbish tip. He roared at the dog and snapped the whip across his back. Bob yelped and hopped. He whipped the dog again and he bolted back to his duties.

The stockman looked back at the little girl and raised his hat. She was crying, huge gulping sobs and a torrent of tears. She stared at him in desperate grief and dashed into the nearest tent. The stockman followed his sheep.

The last couple of miles were steady and he was camped by five o'clock. The sheep were penned and watered. Bob and Meg were fed and chained to a log. His horse was eating from his nose-bag and the saddle was slung over the fence rail. The stockman washed down his damper and corned beef with black tea. He couldn't settle because the little girl's face haunted him. She had seen him whip Bob and she felt she had betrayed the dog. She had seen him whip the dog and she thought him a monster.

The stockman lunged to his feet. He saddled his horse and cantered down the dry, hoof-pocked road. He enjoyed the ride in the cool of the evening with no dust, no flies and no bleating. He and the horse were moving smoothly, drumming along the track. He dismounted a few yards from the tents and dropped the reins; the horse would stand and wait. The woman and child had heard him and they stood outside the tent.

He took off his hat and crouched down until he and girl could see eye to eye. 'Bob has to work for his tucker, little girl. If he gets it into his head to take off and stop working so he can chase other people's rubbish then he'd be no good to me and I'd have to get rid of him. He's a young dog and I have to teach him what's what. I gave that Bob a couple of licks with the whip so as to remind him to get on with the job.' The little girl stared at him and nodded. 'He's resting now, with Meg. I've fed him some mutton and we're square. You don't have to cry about Bob. He knows not to get into rubbish now and I will be able to depend on him. He's my working dog and I need to know he's on the job and I can count on him.' The stockman waited until the child nodded again, grave and gracious, and then he rose to his feet.

He refused the woman's offer of tea but he accepted a large slice of fruitcake wrapped in paper. He made his goodbyes and said he had to get back to the camp. He screwed his hat back onto his head and remounted the horse. He waved to the little girl as he nudged the horse into a walk and the little girl waved back.

A Better Bit of Luck

Why don't you come and stay with me, dear?' said the hair-in-a-bun, floral-dress lady. 'I think your man has had quite a bit to drink. You and your children could have some beds on our verandah.'

Lorrie giggled. She had been giggling and tossing her hands in the air for the last hour. 'My husband,' said Lorrie. 'My husband.' Even after several glasses of champagne Lorrie knew to emphasise the legitimacy of her relationship. She had smarted at the knowledge that there were certain persons in the bush community who had suggested otherwise. Lorrie hiccupped. 'My husband will take us back to camp.' She gave the silent daughter gripping the edge of her bias skirt a small push and instructed her to fetch Kenneth. Lorrie liked to use the lengthy version of Ken's name in dodgy social situations.

Lorrie staggered a little as she turned away from the old busybody to adjust the blanket over the six-month-old baby in the pram. She then leaned over the old sofa and patted the boy sprawled there. He had fallen asleep in the lounge near his mother after a couple of hours of wildly prancing around the hotel and ducking between the legs of stools and men in the bar.

A bit less than half of the seismic party had come into Goondiwindi to The Victoria Hotel, owned by the Pendock family for more than forty-five years, from their camp by Moonie River about seventy miles north. Six drillers, two geophysicists and Lorrie with her three children had made the trip in a two-vehicle convoy. Lorrie had been thrilled because they were going to watch the Melbourne Cup on the television at the Victoria Hotel, a massive structure of about fifty rooms. The Melbourne Cup! It was the most important horse race on the calendar and Lorrie, a true Victorian, believed strongly in marking the day with a bit of pomp.

Lorrie had prepared the baby, she'd dressed the children in clean cotton and then she had insisted they sit still on the camp bed. To aid the achievement of such Mary had agreed to read a story to her brother. Lorrie had had a sponge bath behind the curtain that divided her realm from the rest of the tent. She had put on her dress printed with roses with the full skirt and her nice white shoes. She had fluffed her hair and applied red lipstick. She had known she looked good though Ken's shaving mirror was as much use as a mouse hole in getting an overall view.

This time the trip into town didn't disappoint. Although few had been close enough to the television to see the horses, often a just a fuzz of black and white lines, the radio had boomed the progress of the race. One of the drillers had put his money on Lord Fury. 'I've put m'dosh on the brown horse because it is still a horse. A horse,' he'd loudly maintained, 'will outperform a gelding or a mare, especially when it is only carrying seven and half stone.' Lord Fury had come in four lengths ahead of Grand Print at twenty to one. The exuberant driller, who after the win had even more loudly and drunkenly extolled the virtues of stallions, had bought everyone in the pub a round of beer and demanded the publican open bottles of champagne for the ladies in the lounge.

Lorrie had been thrilled to be included in the celebration and to be the conduit by which the other women in the hotel were able to drink champagne. She had filled her glass several times as she drank a toast to Lord Fury, to the bloody brilliant jockey in the red cap, Ray Selkig, and to the trainer, Frank Lewis, though it was known that his wife had done most of the work on the horse. She had drunk to the success of the drilling and to bloody good mates and to the driller's mother, who was going to get a little something in the post. Lorrie had trilled her delight, laughing immoderately at small amusements, as she had swanned about in the Ladies Lounge all afternoon.

The meal of sausages and egg at five o'clock had gone someway to offset the alcohol consumed but Lorrie was as bright and bold as her husband when it came time to pack up to get back to camp before dark. And so it was that Lorrie shrugged off the offer of hospitality she had so yearned to receive from the insular outback community and simply set off to return to the bush camp in which she lived.

Ken slung his sleeping son over his shoulder and grabbed the basket that contained his baby daughter; both children slept through the rocky transfer to the jeep. The little girl, Mary, guided her mother along the verandah and across the dirt parking lot to the jeep. The departure took a while because Lorrie was gracious in her responses to the verbal flourishes from the drillers and the other drinkers propped against the walls of the pub. Giggles and hand waving subsided once she was inserted into the passenger seat and the baby was placed in her arms. The girl climbed into the back of the jeep. Ken stalled the jeep on its first manoeuvre and the watching drillers jeered and whistled until they were out of sight.

Grog made Ken cautious and the speed of the jeep barely lifted the red dust off the road. The girl watched for the fleeing flicker of monochrome life that populated the side of the road, seeking the sweeter grass from the run off. The family travelled in companionable silence. A tremendous metallic grunt preceded the slew of the jeep across the road and a juddering stop frighteningly close to a red gum. Lorrie's desperate clutch at the baby had squeezed out an angry wail, which was followed by a series of sobs and generous lashings of tears. Lorrie scrabbled her way out of the jeep. She stood patting the baby, whose fear and fright subsided far quicker into quietness than did the galloping thunder of Lorrie's heart. Ken was already on the ground shuffling his shoulders under a vehicle that tilted to the left in demoralising manner. The boy child, re-energised after his sleep, attempted to join his father under the vehicle but retreated after being told in a fierce voice to get out of the bloody way. The girl, whose paleness emphasised her freckles, was put on watch as the disgruntled boy kicked at an ants' nest by the side of the road.

'It could have killed you, Lorrie,' Ken said when he had staggered to his feet. 'Drive shaft has sheared right through and the bloody thing could have shot up through the floor.' The odd mixture of panic and relief in his voice interrupted the children; the boy forgave his father and trotted over and slipped his hand into a greasy, calloused, trembling mitt.

Lorrie swayed. A willi-willi kicked up a fuss on the road and lifted Lorrie's skirt and her spirits. Champagne courage took hold of her tongue, 'Well, I wasn't killed. That's a better bit of luck than winning a few pounds on Lord Fury! Good thing you were going at such a snail's pace, Ken.' She freed a hand from the baby and stroked the pale face of her eldest daughter. 'Now, I think we need a little campfire and a bit of a sing-a-long.'

Throughout the couple of hours that followed she continued to regard the event as one from which she had been saved from dire injury. 'By God, we were lucky,' she repeated this mantra several times as she watched the fire from the comfort of a stool sized rock. The children picnicked on the sultanas and Anzac biscuits which accompanied every outing. Ken played his mouth organ and they sang 'Goodbye Melbourne Town' and 'Speed Bonnie Boat'. Lorrie was saved from having to recognise and properly deal with the inconvenience that had left them stranded by the side of the road by the arrival of the truck carrying the other members of the seismic crew.

Ken waved them down. One by one each man crawled under the broken jeep and assured Ken that he was right and the drive shaft was shot. Each congratulated Lorrie on her close call, who accepted their accolades with a queen-like nod of the head and a giggle. Each patted the nearest child on the back and then stood about rolling smokes and reliving the events of the day and recounting the number of schooners downed. Suddenly the baby gave a demanding cry that had Lorrie staggering to her feet. 'We have to get back to camp,' she informed her husband. Ken assumed his mantle of camp boss and told the men that he would take the truck with Lorrie and the kids back to camp. He would rouse Gordon who would come back and pick up the ones that had to give up their place to his family.

The truck bumped its way along the track and the headlights picked out the grey ashy trunks of the gums. Once a frogmouth was captured in the lights like a huge moth and the flick of a tail and a glint of an eye was all they saw of the shy browsing wallabies. Lorrie sat bolt upright in the cab of the truck. Her head was swimming, the view out of the truck seemed flat and kept sliding away, and she wasn't sure if it was the baby or her stomach squirming. Ken had to help Lorrie from the truck when he pulled up in front of the couple of tents that constituted their home. He left her perched on the front bumper bar, leaning against the cool water bag hooked on the bull bars, while he woke Gordon, who would take the truck back for the rest of the crew, and hunted up a rope for towing the broken-down jeep.

He returned to Lorrie a few minutes later not only with Gordon but Jim as well. The men found Lorrie sitting in the dirt leaning against the wheel of the truck. The baby was wriggling like a worm but Lorrie had a good grip and her eyes were still open. Jim grinned at her. 'Good time, eh, Lorrie?'

Lorrie smiled at him. 'The best,' she said. Then in a puzzled voice she asked to be helped up. 'Why am I sitting on the

Here and There

ground?' she accused Ken. As her husband half carried his wife, who still clutched the baby into the tent, she instructed Jim to bring in the kids asleep in the front of the truck before Gordon went back for the stranded drillers. In the tent Lorrie unbuckled her arms and laid the baby on her bed. Swaying like the kerosene lamp that Ken hurriedly lit and hung from the hook in the ceiling, she supervised the insertion of her son and daughter into the camp beds.

Lorrie's legs suddenly bent like pipe cleaners and tumbled her onto the coir matting. In her ballooning floral frock she looked like she had just got stuck in an overdone curtsy. Lorrie gave a squeal that generated an echo from the now impatient baby. Jim laughed and commented to Ken about one pot screamers. 'She's had quite a few pots, in fact I think she drank the whole damn bottle of champagne on her own,' replied Ken. With Jim's help Ken heaved Lorrie into a sitting position on their bed. Jim took hold of the baby who was getting in a right strop, though the yelling didn't wake the other children. Ken unzipped his wife's dress and pulled off the remaining shoe. Lorrie had lost all shape and hindered Ken's efforts to pull the top of her dress down. Jim had turned delicately away but in the end he had to fix the desperate baby actually on to Lorrie's breast as Ken struggled to keep her in an upright position. Once the changeover to the left breast had been achieved the baby was soon as relaxed as her mother. Lorrie slept through the nappy changing and she was completely unaware of the men debating physics and politics over a few bottles.

Lorrie was late up the next morning because the baby slept in. Ken had taken the other two kids with him up to base camp. She chuckled a bit, as she washed and dressed, sure that her baby had also enjoyed the champagne celebration, albeit via milk. The baby slept on and Lorrie settled at the trestle table for a quiet cup of tea and a couple of boiled eggs.

Lorrie had several drop-ins during the course of the morning. All of them enquired as to about her day out and all of them enquired about her health. Lorrie blithely related the events at the hotel and on the road while she brewed more tea for her pasty visitors. For a couple of the worst afflicted she dug out a few aspirin and, while they rested heavy heads on the camp table, she energetically embarked on the routines of the day.

Here and There

Shoes

Tor's ute creaked when he braked to a stop on Uncle Ralph's drive. Tor sighed at the ominous noise; another visit to Kev and another wodge of dough to cough up to keep the old girl on the road.

Tor was glad to get out of the ute. It was hot. It was particularly hot on the roof of the house he was building. He'd been working in Bargara for more than a week and expected to be on the construction site for about a month more. The job was only a few minutes from where Ralph lived and he had got into the habit of taking his sandwiches to his uncle's place. Uncle Ralph provided tea to wash them down and his house was a damn sight cooler than a rock in the shade of the digger. Also Tor liked the old man. His conversation was measured; his was far easier company than the blokes he was working with whose snappy, one-up-man-ship exchanges really got up his nose.

Tor stretched and swivelled to try and ease the ache that grabbed his lower back. The curse of a Welsh heritage he'd been told. He winced as he leaned into the ute to hook out his sandwich box. He'd toss a couple of aspirin back with his tea and think about buying some serious painkillers on the way home.

As he climbed the open stairs of the old Queenslander he noted a rocking board on the third step. He bounced on it a couple of times and decided that he would replace it before he went back to Bundaberg on Friday. By the time he reached the sixth step he could see Uncle Ralph's shoes and the cuff of his trouser legs. The old man had come out onto the veranda to welcome him. Tor noted, as he did every visit, the high polish on the smart leather shoes and the knife edge pleat of his trousers. Uncle

Here and There

Ralph maintained a high standard of dress. He had not let things slip since Maud died; house and clothes were carefully cared for and properly placed.

Ralph clasped his nephew's shoulder by way a greeting. He waited, while Tor removed his heavy, cement-whitened steel toed boots, and then led the way into the cool shadows of his house.

Ralph and Maud had no children of their own but his brother, who'd died more than ten years ago, had three – the youngest of whom was Tor. Eric and his family had visited often; Bargara's coastal position was pretty attractive to people who lived and worked in the outback. Then Eric's youngsters had grown and gone their own way. Tor's recent return to the area and his visits thrilled Ralph though he was careful not to overwhelm the lad with the intensity of his interest.

Tor handed his lunch box to his uncle. Ralph liked to put the grub on a plate. He would carry the sandwiches to the table on the same tray that brought the heavy metal teapot, a strainer, milk in a jug with a doily to foil the flies, sugar in a blue and white lidded bowl, two white mugs, an embroidered napkin and silver teaspoons. While his uncle busied himself in the kitchen re-boiling the kettle, Tor lowered himself onto the polished wood floor and eased his back against the boards. He hissed through his teeth as the spasms that gripped the muscles in his back relaxed. For a whole two minutes Tor did nothing but enjoy the lack of pain and then he lifted his knees to his chest and rocked gently from side to side. The physio had recommended several other exercises which Tor was again making time for in the morning; he'd been slack about the regime for a few months.

Ralph had returned with the lunch. From his prone position Tor got a longer and closer look at those brown polished, slip-on shoes. The leather was the same colour as well-kept saddle. They looked soft and expensive. Tor remembered his mother saying that Ralph spent more on his shoes than Maud did.

Tor levered himself to his feet and sat carefully on the chair. Ralph placed his plate of sandwiches and a napkin in easy reach and then began turning the pot. It was a ritual of three clockwise and three anticlockwise turns. Ralph said it settled the tea leaves and improved the brew. He poured milk and then the black tea into the large mugs. He added three teaspoons of sugar to Tor's cup and placed it and a teaspoon in front of the lad.

'Do you miss riding and farming?' Tor asked his uncle. The soft shoes were still in his mind and he wondered what the old man thought of the harder life and the tougher footwear of his youth.

'I was never much of a rider, Tor. Not like your father who loved the horses. I liked going by car, even preferred Shanks's pony to riding. I was glad to give up the droving. Seven years on a horse covered in dust or mud tends to cure a man of the romance of riding.'

'But Dad said you were good with the horses.'

'I tended to them. Looked after their feet and made sure their tack fitted easy and snug. Less likely he'll spill you in the dust, then. I did a bit of blacksmithing if it were required. Even so, I found the riding hard yakka. I was glad when I had earnt enough to buy the farm and could pack the droving in.'

The two men sat quietly and Tor ate his sandwiches. Ralph refilled Tor's cup from the pot. Tor thought about how very different Ralph was from his brother. Eric had always harked back to his droving days and had spoken of the long rides mustering cattle with yearning and affection. Over the years his father had told and retold his son various stories about the men and horses who'd worked bloody-minded cattle and bloody stupid sheep. Eric always wore R.M. Williams riding boots, especially when he went to town in Camooweal, even though he didn't keep a horse on the dairy farm; well not after old Yarraman had died.

Here and There

'Dad told me that you straightened a horseshoe with your bare hands,' Tor offered to Ralph. This story had been circulating in the family for years and Tor was glad to have an opportunity to get the truth from the horse's mouth.

Ralph laughed. 'My hands were tough and my shoulders were solid when I was your age. Yeah, I straightened a horseshoe, but it was still pretty hot from the fire and it belonged to the smallest horse on the drive. Eric won a bit of money from that stunt. The other drovers talked it up to save face about being bilked out of some of their drinking money. It's the sort of thing that you'd only do once, if you've got any sense; puts too much of a strain on the body.' Ralph paused. 'And people get too excited and have expectations.'

Tor nodded. He'd seen that in action himself. Aunt Maud had been another who had spread the word about the strength of Ralph's arm. A brash trucker from Gladstone had come to the local dance and listed his arm wrestling achievements to all who'd listen and even to those who would rather not. Maud had been trapped behind the table serving scones and, worn down by the bloke's boasting, she had snapped that she was sure her husband would be the better man when it came to arm wrestling.

The words were like a red rag to a bull and within a few moments Ralph had been hustled from his comfortable position by the bar and sat at a table opposite the red-faced man from Gladstone. Maud had placed her hand briefly on Ralph's shoulder and stepped back. Tor, who'd been about ten at the time, wormed his way to the front of the mob that gathered about the contest. It was mostly men and they urged Ralph to uphold the honour of the locals. It had been a quick and ruthless contest. Ralph had pushed the stranger's hand to the boards of the table twice. Tor remembered how, each time, as he took the strain of the other man's push, the white shoulder of Ralph's shirt had bulged and stretched. He remembered the tremor in the Gladstone man's arm and then the guttural groan of the loser as his hand hit the table.

Ralph had escaped the congratulations of the locals, presented brief commiserations to the loser, who'd kept offering to manage him at the next round of arm-wrestling contests, and went looking for Maud. Tor had dogged his uncle as he had made his way across the wooden floor to his wife. He watched as Maud kissed him on the cheek and patted that tough hand then she had placed her hand on his shoulder and they'd danced. Maud was on the square side and so was Ralph but he remembered how they sailed like galleons on the dance floor. Majestically, they had circled the Town Hall and Maud had shone, like a shiny bronze figure of victory, in Ralph's careful arms which were once more properly clad in his jacket.

Tor's lunch hour was almost done. He excused himself from the table and went down the corridor to the dunny. Ralph had left his bedroom door open and Tor glanced in and paused. Under the white painted dressing table were two pairs of shoes. One pair of polished black lace-ups nestled close to a pair of bronze court shoes.

Here and There

A Particularly Long Absence

Maggie woke with a keen sense of anticipation. She got out of her double bed quickly ignoring the twinges and aches that beset her every move. After she had washed at the basin, she put on her striped dress. The one Dan liked. She frowned at its fit, gaping somewhat around the top and a bit tight in the middle, because she had thought that it was flattering and comfortable. Despite how the push of excitement made her hands tremble she took the time to apply a little colour to her cheeks and lips.

Throughout breakfast, during the clearing of the table and while she was washing up, Maggie ran through Dan's movements. She knew that he would have finished that inland long haul shift and he would have got the truck to the depot in the city late in the evening. He wouldn't have called if it was after ten and Maggie also knew that the phones at the depot were not very well maintained. Once at the depot he would do as many checks as he could by the security lights. Then he would sleep.

Maggie shivered with pleasure as she continued rehearsing his routine in the morning. Like her, Dan would have risen early in the morning. While she was washing her dishes he would have been washing his truck. After that he would finish the checks and time sheets. Maggie looked out of the kitchen window at the scalped garden. She was surprised that Dan was permitting his precious vegetable patch to be absorbed by the lawn.

She frowned.

Maggie had put away the dishes and brushed the kitchen floor. The linoleum was beginning to wear in some patches though it was not that obvious in the dark green geometric pattern. She and Dan would discuss getting some new when he got home. She looked at the gold carriage clock on the bureau, a wedding gift that still kept excellent time, and realised that Dan would be about his breakfast at the canteen. She knew he took his time in the morning sharing yarns about near misses, road kill and the bloody idiots he and the other truckers had to endure on the roads. Soon though he would be at the office to hand in his schedule and wait for clearance. Once that happened, Maggie hugged herself but only for a moment as her shoulders protested, he would retrieve his car from the secure lock-up and drive home. A trip which usually took around two hours and, if things went smoothly, he would be turning right onto Lower Lake Road shortly after eleven.

Maggie heard the clock strike the hour and she put away the dusting cloth and hastened into the front room. She angled the cane bottom chair so that she could see out of the window and hooked the lace curtain aside so that she had an unimpeded view. Maggie settled her bones carefully on to the cushions, surprised by how lean and meagre was the flesh on her buttocks and shanks. She panted a little because the roll of fat around her middle and the tight waist of the striped dress impinged on her breathing. She plucked at the striped dress in an effort to make it sit more comfortably.

Maggie lived in a small weatherboard house near the corner of one of many roads out of the town. Directly opposite her vantage point, the cars came to a standstill at the T-junction before turning left to more rural properties or right to the lake. She knew that the junction was busy during the get-to-work and time-for-school hours. It was as busy in the late afternoon with the same cars rushing for the comforts of home. But Maggie wasn't interested in those times of day; she only sat by the window between eleven and twelve fifteen.

Maggie was waiting for Dan.

She leaned in, close to the glass of the window, every time a car approached the junction and prepared to pull up at the stop sign. If the flicker of the oncoming car was signalling right her heart picked up pace to match the flashing light. The driveway of the house was immediately off Lower Lake Road. Dan would signal right and then signal left to pull into their driveway.

She studied each driver carefully. She had a blank about the model and colour because Dan changed his car every five years. His very own five-year plan he would joke. Good thing his face was so distinctive and Maggie smiled to think she would be giving that dear face a kiss very soon.

It was a dull day and the drivers were neither wearing sunglasses nor squinting which made their faces easier to see. Sometimes a driver would catch sight of her, nose almost on the window pane, and give her a wave. Maggie would courteously wave back with a queenly hand, even though she had already lost interest because it was clearly not her Dan, and she waited impatiently for the next car.

When the clock struck twelve, Maggie began, reluctantly, to inch herself out of the chair. She dawdled through the moves that took her to her feet. Once upright she shook the down cushions so they filled their chintz covers and she pulled the lace curtains back into place fussing over their sepia folds. She eased the striped dress into a better shape on her standing body.

At two Maggie spread the uneaten lunch on the grass near the back door. The crows and magpies took the meat and the more colourful birds scratched and pecked at the vegetables. They had come to expect this largess and in the moment before she flung the food to the ground it was as if she were in the eye of a storm of calls and feathers.

Usually Maggie would be calmly resigned to a delay. She knew he would not be home today; the routine was fixed. This time, though, this time she felt the pressure of her disappointment rise up as if it might choke her. She was used to Dan's trucking contracts keeping him away from home for days but this one had seemed to have taken him on a particularly long journey.

Maggie leant against the sink as she placed the empty plate into the plastic wash basin. She was breathing as heavily as if she had just run a race rather than walked across the linoleum of the utility and kitchen. She felt a tear ooze onto her cheek. Waiting in the house was no longer endurable.

Maggie put on her coat. It was a warm, spring day but she was unaware of such external considerations. She was totally focussed on exiting her lonely home. She found her black handbag and left. It wasn't until she was standing at the bus stop that she realised she still had on her slippers and her pinafore. The prompt arrival of the bus distracted her from going back home to change.

In town Maggie sought the solace of the enclosed shopping centre. The air conditioning hummed and the canned music thrummed as if the bright window displays had a voice as well as a look. Maggie pressed a hand, strange how that hot hard light made it look a bit misshapen, against the glass of the jewellery shop and sighed over the hard glitter of the diamonds and the gleam of the lesser gems. She breathed a fog of appreciation onto the window of the lighting shop as she admired the Tiffany lamps.

Maggie turned to proceed further into shopping centre, she always liked seeing the display of the buttons and bows of the haberdashery, and she saw Dan. She was engulfed with the joy of seeing him. He looked so well and strong. No trace of his 'trucker's belly'. He must have kept to that diet the doctor had suggested for him. Maggie felt a brief wave of guilt that she had cooked up sausages and mash for his lunch.

She called out.

'Dan. Dan!' He looked at her. She could see that he was shocked to see her. Actually he looked appalled. Maggie felt her heart plummet. Dan began to walk quickly towards her. A pretty young woman accompanied him. 'Dan, where have you been? I waited and waited for you.'

Any answer given was swamped by the realisation that the young woman, dressed far too skimpily for decency, was holding onto Dan's arm. Holding on to her Dan's arm!

Maggie gave a cry of rage and tried to smack the woman. She felt Dan prevent her hand from falling on that smooth face.

'Don't. Don't,' he said. 'It's Cathy. It's my wife. Don't hit her.'

'Wife, wife,' Maggie turned her rage on to Dan. 'How can you have a wife? You have me. You have me!' Maggie was gripped by a dreadful realisation. 'Is that why you have been away on such long journeys? Is that why I have been left alone?' She could hear Dan speaking but his words didn't penetrate the roaring in her ears. Her heart was hammering. 'What about us. What about the children?' Maggie was banging her fist on the arm that restrained her. 'How could you be with her when I was waiting for you? How could you be with her when I made lunch for you?'

Maggie's wails were attracting attention. The arm around her tightened and she could hear Dan's gasps and gulps as he began to guide her out of the shopping centre. For a moment she was silent and she could hear Cathy making high pitched coaxing noises. 'This way, Maggie, come along. We'll go home and have a nice cup of tea. A cup of tea and we will sort it all out.' She cried out louder in despair and pain.

Suddenly she was aware that she was outside. The sky had cleared and the sun was warm and casting shadows on to the pavement. She could feel Dan, still with his arms around her, shaking. Dan was speaking in a trembling voice. 'Oh, please, don't. Don't. Don't go on.' Maggie stopped struggling, stopped shouting and stopped crying. She felt as if she had been hollowed out. She was weak with the horror of Dan's betrayal. 'It's me, Pete. I'm Peter, Mum. Oh Mum. Come now, I'll take you home and we will talk about Dad when we get there.'

W Lodwick Lowdon

The Haunting

Macka scowled at the petrol gauge. It was hovering just above the red and he still had at least forty klicks to go to reach his small holding in Maryborough.

He cursed his luck all over again. He'd chosen to bypass the Shell service station in favour of better deal at BP further down the road but had found out they closed at nine on a Sunday night. In fact the whole of Sunday could be classified as a bloody poor show; one bloody piece of mismanagement after another.

Macka's scowl deepened as he recalled the rugby match. He'd copped a few too many tackles early in the game which had slowed him down but it was no excuse for making two late tackles and giving away two successful penalty kicks. Macka shifted in his seat and felt his left leg flare with pain. One of those Melbourne bastards had stomped on him during a muddy scramble for the ball; a bloke would have to be a saint to think it was anything but deliberate. But, as he hadn't been flavour of the month in the dressing room after the match, there was little sympathy from a team nursing bruises and bruised pride.

No sympathy from Rhonda either. Her temper had been curdled by the mud and the damp. She'd ended up sitting in the car with a smelly wet dog reading an out-of-date paper unable to distinguish the teams due to smears on the windscreen and all of the players being dressed in blotchy brown shirts. By the time Macka had got to the car she was frantically filing her nails. 'To stop myself from chewing my hand off,' she'd informed Macka. She was well launched into full whinge mode. In fact they both were.

The pub in St Kilda had served good tucker but Rhonda's moans about a new IT system and her messy flatmate interrupted by Macka's grumbles about the latest ploughing contract had not complemented the meal. Even the wine had tasted thin and flat. They had tried to get into a better mood by walking along the esplanade. Milly, with the optimism that was characteristic of a kelpie, had enjoyed the walk but not Rhonda and Macka, who had continued carping at each other. The new moon had only appeared a couple of times out of thick cloud and then it had just been a sliver; a pinched metaphor for their romance.

Rhonda hadn't invited Macka home and Macka was shockingly relieved. They'd fumbled their parting kiss in the car park of the apartment block, where Rhonda lived, and their 'See you later' had been less than heartfelt. He'd let Milly out of the car for a break and watched her shit on the lawn with no compunction whatsoever. She had been the only one wagging a tail on this sorry, soggy Sunday.

Macka shook his head to clear it from remembering the dross of the day and he looked in his rear vision mirror at his dog spread-eagled on the back seat; how the hell she'd managed to talk herself out of the back of the station wagon he still didn't know. He angled the mirror back into its proper place and saw only black.

The fuel gauge was now firmly in the red. Like his bank balance! Macka dragged his thoughts away from that abyss and looked at the clock and was shocked to see less than ten minutes had passed. He began seriously to worry about whether he would make it home before the car conked out. Usually he travelled with a can of petrol but he'd taken it out when he'd given the car a bit of a spruce up for Rhonda. He scowled again. What a disaster of a day. The potential embarrassment of having to hitch a lift to get fuel really gnawed at Macka. Every bush kid knew not to travel without reserves and here was one in his late twenties about to have to spend the night by the side of the road because he didn't put enough petrol in his tank.

Macka tried to laugh at himself but he ached and he felt slow, even old. He just didn't fancy being stuck in the middle of Victoria in the dark on his tod. Well, he had Milly and, as if she'd read his thoughts, she slapped her tail a few times on the seat.

He welcomed the signs announcing Dunolly. He reduced his 'conserve petrol' speed to below the fifty klicks requested as he entered the town and dropped out of high beam as a courtesy.

'Town!' Macka scoffed at such a word to describe Dunolly. 'Skeletown, more like,' he said aloud to the dog. Driving through the broken-down remnants of the gold rush always gave Macka the creeps. The sagging clapboard houses with dirty yellow lace curtains, wide pot-holed streets owned by a couple of feral dogs and street signs used for target practice were not encouraging in broad daylight. It was hard to believe that in the late 1850s there'd been sixty thousand turning earth, tunnelling into rock and scrabbling for gold and survival in this ruined land. Macka knew there were less than two hundred people living in Dunolly now and none of them were about after midnight. The place was dead: not a soul stirring and not a light burning.

Macka looked at the dashboard. The needle was on the bottom line. Still, once he was through Dunolly, it was only another fifteen klicks and he'd be home. He felt positive for the first time that day. Macka slowed to a crawl at the stop sign in the town centre and turned left to take a shortcut to Maryborough Road.

Suddenly he felt very, very sure there was someone sitting in the seat directly behind him. He heard Milly whimper and then he felt her ooze through the gap between the front seats and crawl onto the floor.

Macka fixed his eyes on the road. The dipped headlights framed the black tarmac edged by a wide sandy and quartz runoff. The ruined buildings of the old town covered a large area. He crept along the wide streets at thirty kilometres per hour. He didn't look in the mirror and he'd be damned if he'd turn around. The presence behind him was not friendly, not friendly at all.

By the light of the dashboard he could see Milly was curled into a tight ball with her tail tucked up. Macka felt a huge desire to assume the same foetal position. His granite grip on the steering wheel was getting slippery with sweat. The hair on his neck prickled and he eased himself forward, away from the back of his seat and the proximity of his uninvited passenger.

Macka kept his eyes on the dark road. He was convinced his only hope lay in not acknowledging his passenger. To look to see who was there meant being looked at. To admit it was there would be to admit a whole lot more. His legs were beginning to cramp. Meg whined and curled herself into a smaller size. Macka clenched his teeth on his own whine and prayed the car wouldn't stop. He had a very, very bad feeling about stopping.

Macka took the left-hand turn onto the Maryborough Road without slowing down; a big looping corner which had the car kicking up dust from both sides of the road. He wished for a copper to pull him over. He prayed all over again that the car would not stop and he prayed the petrol would last a bit longer. He flicked up the high beam. The road ahead was straight and black and headlights sparked off the orange cat's eyes fixed in the centre of the tarmac. Macka knew the land around was barren, full of holes and mullock heaps. It was literally the dead end of a dying town.

As suddenly as it arrived it went. The passenger, the pressure of its presence, was gone. The rigid man and the cowering dog began to assume softer lines. Macka unlocked his jaw and groaned with relief. Milly climbed onto the front seat and he ruffled her neck with a shaking hand.

'We'll be home in a jiffy,' he croaked to his dog. 'And next time we'll travel by way of Castlemaine and skip the damned Dunolly shortcut.'

The Old Dog

The three young gap-year students stopped talking in their round brass voices when the old man sat at their table, uninvited. They hadn't had time to take more than a couple of mouthfuls from the beers in front of them. Well, he wasn't that old. He was in his forties with weathered dark skin, sinewy arms and calloused hands, which he spread on the table. He looked tough and, worse, he looked angry.

'It was Sunday arvo' and I was in the garage,' his voice was harsh and intense. 'Annie was playin' in our front yard. I thought by the sound that a few motorbikes were revving their engines as they went by our place. But that wasn't what was goin' on. It was that bastard makin' a couple of passes, checkin' out if Annie was alone.'

The young men stared at the interloper in astonishment. His khaki shirt was stained; they could see the top of his hairy chest and he smelt of work.

'I know there's trouble when Jaspar started makin' a hell of a racket; a barrage of barks that tells me there's a snake. I was out of that garage in a flash but I was too slow. I couldn't see Annie. I sort of dithered. Ran backwards and forwards with me heart chokin' me.'

The big, rough hands clenched and unclenched a couple of times and the gap-year students stared at them. There was a whisper travelling around the pub and somebody had turned off Slim Dusty. The man continued to speak. 'My little girl had just up and disappeared. But Jaspar was barking at the gate, pawing and butting at the steel mesh. And that's when I saw a motorbike headin' away north along the tarmac road and it had somethin' yellow hangin' down the side of the fuel tank.'

One of the young men, with sun chapped lips, stopped mid-reach for his beer when the table crasher shook his head. 'I was crazy for a bit and raced out into the road and began to run after that bike. As if a man on foot would be able to catch a motorbike!' Chapped lips swallowed his smile when the brown eyes in the grim face glared at him.

'Jaspar brought me to my senses. He was sniffing about and then began to follow that bike in a determined manner. He was on a trail. I realised that there were splatters and drops of blood on the road. That bastard must have hurt Annie, bashed her nose or gashed her arm or something haulin' her onto the front of his bike. And I could smell piss. Poor little tyke had wet herself with fear and pain when he grabbed her.'

The speaker paused and looked down at the table. The three students, flushed with youth and arrogance and an excess of sun, exchanged quick glances. The biggest lad, the one wearing a denim shirt, twirled a finger around his right ear and shuffled his feet as if he was going to stand up. 'You just sit there 'til I tell you otherwise,' growled the man. The restless youth froze. The squeak of the limping fan filled the room. It was late afternoon and the patches of sunlight on the wooden floor were shrinking.

'I raced back to the garage and heaved out the quad bike. It is a horrible thing when you pray that your daughter keeps on drippin' blood or wee so that your dog can track her.

'By the time I caught up with Jasper he'd already travelled a couple of clicks. I tracked him as he followed those blood spots along the road from our place. It was close to midday and pretty hot but the speedo on the quadbike told me that Jasper was sometimes moving at about fifteen klicks an hour. I was starting to panic cos I could see the dog was slowing down; there was a bloody paw print now and again. Then, about seven klicks from our place, the dog picked up where the motorbike had turned off the main road.'

The man stopped talking while he considered the nightmare of missing that turn. Apart from the fan there was not a sound in the pub.

'It was tarmac for a bit and then we were travelled along an old mining track. The bloody quad bike ran out of juice so I ditched her and I was back to being on foot again. Jaspar kept finding somethin' to follow and I stuck to that dog like a burr. We wasted a couple of minutes at the foot of a ridge where the gravel road divided and the bike had chewed up the ground but Jaspar scouted about and took the left fork and within a couple of hundred metres I could see the tyre tracks in the dust.'

Now all the students were beginning to twitch on their plastic chairs. Their beer was going flat. 'Hey mister, we don't want to listen anymore.' The man shoved the round table so it pushed into their bellies and they sat still.

'What's the matter with you?' the tall, thin lad in expensively ripped jeans and limited edition T-shirt gasped out.

'Listen. Just you shut up and listen.' He gave the table another bit of a shove and beer slopped onto its dark green Masonite surface. The young men were really uncomfortable now and looked around for a bit of support.

'What's this all about?' the thin student asked the room at large. All three lads looked hopefully at the several men bunched around the bar. The locals, who were watching the tense scene carefully, responded to the question with head shakes and sneers; one, strategically placed at the end of the bar close to the wooden and glass door, gave them the finger. The young men sat still and stiff.

'When we arrived in that little gully, the disgusting bastard was shruggin' himself out of his leathers. He was stripped down to his waist and was beginnin' to work on the trousers. Annie was sittin' in a heap at his feet. Her yellow T-shirt was bloody and dirty and she was crying. She had on one sandal and her toes were scraped and bleeding. Jasper and I had seen the other one lying in the road only about five hundred metres from home.'

'Jaspar got to the bastard first. He ripped a hole in his arm so deep that I could see the white of the bone before the blood started pouring. That bastard only had time for a couple of screams before I smashed him over the head with a large piece of wood. I gave him a few more wallops while he was on the ground but I stopped because Jaspar was worryin' his face and throat and I didn't want to risk hitting the dog.'

'By the time I had patted Annie down, hugged her, cried and carried her out of sight of the action in the gully, Jaspar had chewed that bastard to death.'

The table shuddered. The whole room sat in silence. The three young men held their breath. They were beginning to wonder if it was a bit of a wind-up and the biggest one leaned back a bit in his chair.

'Once I calmed down I siphoned petrol out of the tank of the motorbike into the jerry can he had taped on the back to fuel the quad bike. And we rode home. I had my left arm wrapped around Annie where she sat in front of me and Jaspar balanced on the back of the quad bike.'

The stocky man stopped talking. The big one, who thought he knew the lay of the land, opened his mouth to speak but shut it when the man leaned in close pushing hard against the table.

'That was six years ago and Jaspar is an old dog now. His teeth are blunt, his hair is more white than brindle, and there's no way he'd cover a klick let alone ten. He just lies down. He's lyin' down on the verandah out there.' The muscles under his stained shirt bulged as he flicked his thumb over his shoulder at the entrance.

'And you kicked him.' The man leaned forward and poked a thick finger into the T-shirt of the stylish lad. 'Yeah, you! He poked the youth harder. You're a nasty piece of work! I saw you put the boot in m' dog as you came into the pub.' He poked the trembling youth a couple more times, hard and fierce jabs. 'And you lily-livered lot,' his voice was full of disgust as he looked at the other two, 'You thought kicking an old dog was funny.' Chapped lips and denim shirt dropped their heads to avoid the glare of his outrage.

The tough sinewy man gave the table a vicious shove as he stood up and the beers toppled and spilled over the table and onto the laps of the mortified gap-year students.

'You're a bunch of bloody useless, cruel buggers and we don't want your type around here. Get out of this pub and get out of this town or I'll make sure you join that bastard in the gully. Go on, piss off, the lot of ya. I'll tell Jonsie that you've quit and done a runner.'

The New Car

Janine bought a new car when she was twenty-three.

Initially she felt pretty self-important about being an owner of an object worth thousands of dollars until she realised how firmly it tied her, tied her right and tight, to the job. Three years at the chalk face, overseen by Sister Margaret and patronised by Pastor John who were attempting to develop an ecumenical educational vision in rural Victoria, to get close to paying it off. Janine, yet again, was beholden to the parents because they coughed up for the substantial deposit.

Janine was very and really grateful that they had agreed to lend her the money except she had to, frequently, demonstrate a lively sense of favours bestowed and received. This expectation of gratitude was heightened when her mother's mother was visiting; Janine wished she spoke several languages so she could reduce the blandness of the 'thank you' that was repeatedly requested and expressed.

Yet she was so very glad to have that car.

For the first few months of the school year Janine lived in town and walked to school. Then she and Heather moved out of the fishbowl to a farmhouse about eight kilometres out of Maryborough and she used to get a lift to work with her housemate. She would put a bit in for the petrol; she got most of her marking done hanging around waiting for Heather, a charismatic teacher, to finish doling out wisdom and netball tactics to her students. Then Heather met a man! She was away to Melbourne for the whole weekend, every weekend. Without a car Janine was marooned in a flinty yellow scrubby landscape with her dog.

To avoid the knotty emotional and fiscal indebtedness to her parents, Janine had considered cycling into town. It was not an idea she entertained for very long as it would take over half an hour and involve the couple of hills between the clapboard farmhouse to Maryborough; then there was the consideration that temperature was more than thirty degrees for six months out of the ten.

A very unpleasant episode with the bloke who delivered a bookcase and returned later the same night with a mate underlined how isolated Janine felt. If it weren't for Kim, she had growled so savagely at the unwanted visitors that foam dripped from her jaws, Janine felt it might have gone rather badly. Kim's bared teeth had added gravitas to Janine's shrill injunction to both men, screamed through the flimsy fly screen door, that they 'piss off or she would bloody well call the police'. Janine's heart still stuttered when she thought about it. She was pretty keen after that to get some wheels because a car would reduce the sitting duck feeling.

The new car was green and a Mazda. The first characteristic displeased her mother as she was superstitious about green cars and the second really curdled her father's attitude as he was anti-Japanese. This may explain why Janine ended up paying interest to her parents for the loan at the same level as she would have done to a bank. The sole advantage to having to repay her parents was that they would only bend her ear if she was late with a repayment.

Janine loved her car. 'I called her Jade,' she would tell her friends. They looked at her blankly. 'Pretty damn witty name when you add in all the connotations.' It only created more incomprehension. 'You know. My car is like the colour of the precious stone but it also means a horse and a wild woman.'

'Janine,' they would say with a double drag on the last vowel in her name, similar to the emphasis her grandmother used more often than not, when she tried to share the cleverness of the moniker for her steed. Janine stopped talking about her little witticism but she privately acknowledged Jade's service with a pat every time she got in or out of her beloved car.

Once Janine had wheels she could do stuff.

She joined the local netball team. Janine considered herself a savvy and fast player but she almost packed it in after her first evening of training. The other members of the team pulled up in utes and bashed up Holdens. Before they went on the court a couple of them took out their teeth; the disappearance of their lips and the subsequent black holes when they shouted was very off-putting. Women's netball, Janine quickly learnt, was tough and stapled to local pride. 'If you're not going to commit don't bother turning up.' Janine stuck with it and wore her bruises with some pride.

Janine drove to nearby towns. She liked Castlemaine. There were a couple junk shops that occasionally dragged some money out of her pocket and the Jiffy Tea Shop made the best malted milkshakes in Victoria. Now and again she would take Jade on a spin to Maldon and marvel at how the influx of arty shops was transforming the old gold town from month to month. She took particular pleasure in clomping along the wooden verandahs and crossing the wide high streets in her riding boots.

While she was in Maryborough Janine learnt to ride a horse. With Jade she could get to the riding lessons organised by her friend, the art teacher. She handed over a few dollars each week for the privilege but the real payment turned out to be posing for a picture, 'Woman Ironing'. Janine reckoned she must have pressed every piece of cloth owned by Martha and her family at least three times! Her mother really disliked the portrait because she thought it was unrealistic. 'You hate ironing and you definitely don't press shirts correctly,' she would complain every time she saw the portrait.

Janine put away the riding boots when she drove down to Melbourne and relished giving her flamboyant shirts and skirts an outing. Most of her university friends had scattered but she'd meet Tracy at Melbourne Art Gallery and afterwards they would eat at one of the Italian restaurants in Carlton. They'd walk the length of Lygon Street, appreciating the posturing of the young men draped over their highly polished cars with fluff on the back window shelves, before they chose their place to eat. All the restaurants were BYO and they'd take turns in bringing the wine; Janine would drink one large gorgeous glass of red, Tracy would drink two and take the rest home to Bertie.

That car, the mighty Jade, took Janine on a tour of the Great Ocean Road. When Janine drove that road there were nine apostles standing. She thought the Southern Ocean had done away with three before she had got there but a bit of research revealed that there were only ever nine since navigators marked them on a map.

Once she drove Pat, who'd recently lost his licence, to the edge of the Otway National Park. They stayed a couple of days with one of his mates, Bluey Smith. Bluey was a Vietnam veteran. Throughout Saturday afternoon tough, edgy men, who'd also served in the war, trickled down from their retreats in the mountains usually arriving on black motorbikes. Janine couldn't help but stare when Bluey used the opener soldered onto his peg leg to flick the caps off the beer. They were cynical men, impatient with her romantic bullshit view of the world, so Janine spent most of her time with Bluey's mother. They sat together at the kitchen table playing cribbage. While she played, Bluey's mother propped her huge breasts on the kitchen table to take the weight off her back. Janine was bereft when the truckie came, Bluey's mother was a Justice of the Peace, and took her away for a whole afternoon to do her stuff for him at the local police station.

One school break saw Janine drive Jade to Port Fairy via the Grampians. She collected Annie, who'd managed to wrangle time off for the same week, from Melbourne airport and they went travelling. At Hall's Gap in the Grampians Annie took the nerve test, she stepped the not-quite-a-metre from one craggy outcrop onto the Pinnacle while Janine watched from the ridge, unable to walk the spine let alone make the step. They set up their tent in a rough mowed paddock outside Port Fairy. They would spend the day driving to different places but returned to camp before dark. Three evenings in a row they made the short walk from the dingy Southcombe camping ground to Griffiths Island and three heart-wrenching times Janine and Annie watched the mutton birds scimitar out of the Southern Ocean and slice into the burrows at their feet. On the last night in the campsite Janine slept with a knife underneath her sleeping bag. She told Annie it was a comfort when the drunks in the tent nearby kicked off but Annie thought Janine's solution was more worrying that the noise next door.

In the summer Janine would drive to Brisbane and stay with her mum and dad; three and a half thousand kilometres for a round trip through the Eastern States of Australia. Big trips! Oh the parents would volunteer to pay for flights but Janine declined. The journey was a major joy and she didn't want to leave her dog, Kim, behind. Besides, being stuck in a Brisbane suburb with no transport was not ideal, especially if her grandmother was also present.

Janine was happy with just her dog for company for those long drives. Teaching involved interaction with other people all the time; sharing a house included compromises and collective decisions; and staying with her parents meant biting her tongue a lot. Driving Jade along the inland highway was real freedom; she liked being the only person she had to please.

Often she would diverge from the main route even though and because it made it a longer journey.

Sometimes Janine would park the car by a dry riverbed. Sometimes she would bump down a siding until she was a couple of kilometres from the main road and put up her tent. Sometimes she would just throw down a swag under an ancient tree. She tended not to camp too near water as she was a martyr to mosquitoes but also because that was where she was most likely to meet a snake. Once Kim and Janine had played statues for a full ten minutes while a tiger snake drank at the billabong where she was filling her billy. Wherever they had chosen to camp, the exuberant shrieks of parrots and parakeets, the open joyous chuckles of the kookaburras and the shrill whistles and warbles of the smaller birds would catapult them from the tent at dawn. They'd take a bit of walk along the track, inevitably spook the local wallabies and kangaroos, and then they'd leave.

If the weather was unfavourable they would stay in pubs. Pubs were pretty relaxed about dogs and Kim could sleep on a mat in the room. The rooms were usually upstairs and had large windows that looked onto a verandah. They were big rooms with high ceilings studded by a large dusty fan which, as often as not, did not work. The floors and the furniture were wooden and painted and chipped. The beds were always covered by a candlewick quilt and there would be bleached copies of Albert Namajirra's gumtrees on the wall. The facilities were shared and approached along dark corridors.

Janine would eat and drink in the lounge after a beer at the bar. Now and again she'd get into conversation with a local and pick up some info about a natural feature or a dog trial or bit of a do at a racecourse. She would trade the book she'd finished reading for a battered novel found on a wonky bookcase and retire to her room. Around ten at night, Kim and Janine would wander about the sleeping town, rural communities went to bed early, and enjoy the cool air listening to the rustle and croak of the nocturnal animals.

Janine sold the car in 1983. She sold Jade to Heather's brother, Max, who worked as a psychiatric nurse at Thomas Embling Hospital for the criminally insane. The money he paid financed two months' overseas travel and Janine left for Europe in late December. The trip met none of her expectations. She went to Edinburgh, London, Paris and Madrid but in each city it was bloody cold, it was dark before four o'clock and few of the big attractions were open. Janine spent more time than she had planned in art galleries and overspent her budget on staying warm by watching dubious productions in theatres.

Janine knew she should have kept the car.

Lightning Ridge

The silver surfers in their hire 4X4 drew up beside me. Well, they were a bit more polite than that and parked a courteous four metres from my truck. I was lazing away the heat of the day by my red Toyota under the only decent sized tree on this stretch of the mining track. I was still on the water; I make it a rule not to slug a beer until dusk. Too many blokes around here are comatose and useless by mid-morning. Also, I was contemplating hitting the road and getting out of Lightning Ridge; besides, the local cops were pretty sharp on drink driving.

Neither one of the couple turned out to be anything special when they climbed out of their dusty jeep. He was middle height, wiry, with a bit of a pot belly; and, I'd bet my bottom dollar, he was bald under that brown leather hat. She was a solid sheila but still with a bit of shape to her. She had dyed black hair; a colour that I reckon was a decade out of date and her eyes flashed blue when she looked at me while shoving a straw hat on her head. As soon as she saw I was looking right back at her she walked over to me. Her husband, they were both packing gold wedding rings, followed on behind. Seeing those rings gave me a pang. I had to ditch mine a few months ago along with the cheating bitch who'd given it to me.

'You look like you know what you to do around here.' She was direct and uncomplicated. 'We thought that we'd like a shot at fossicking for opals but we've not much of an idea about how to go about it. Are we at the right mullock heaps as we don't want to tread on anyone's toes?'

I liked her caution. Opal miners protected their rights aggressively in Lightning Ridge. They didn't like tourists or fly-bys near their claims and were as vigilant about the dirt they'd discarded as they were about the mounds that were yet to be examined. Her bloke explained to me that they had driven around the diggings and that one of the miners had told them that they could fossick in the mullock heaps of the big company mining group.

They were an easy, likable couple. They looked at me as if I mattered and as if I was a font of wisdom. Flattering. Especially for a man who hadn't had anyone pay him much attention for bit. Sure I go to the pub and exchange words with the other fossickers and miners but we all take on interchangeable parts: 'How are ya, mate? It's been a hot one! Want another? Did ya catch the footy/racing/cricket action? Have a smoke.' To which a bloke answers, 'Yeah', 'all right', 'no (low on money and don't want to get into a shout)', 'no' and 'no'. Occasionally I find out that so-and-so has packed it in and gone south or that some blow-in has staked a claim on in the Eastern section of the Ridge.

I looked in my mug. The couple of inches of water remaining were covered by a thin patina of white dust. The vehicles kicked up most of it but even walking created a mist around your feet and legs. I chucked the water onto the trunk of the tree and we began to talk about opal fossicking.

'Now and again, too rarely for everyone's hopes,' I answered another question. 'A miner will show a few opals packed in cotton wool in a cigarette tin. He'll hawk them to the tourists first and if that doesn't work go down to the assessor and see what he can gouge out of him. Harder work than mining trying to get a decent price for opals.'

There's thousands of miners live around Lightning Ridge; mostly men, a handful of women, a few couples and even fewer families,' I told them. We had moved into the skimpy shade of damaged gum beside my rig. The woman had gone over and fetched a large bottle of ginger beer and a bowl of olives. Olives! Nice, but.

'Yet the damn funny thing is that there are only one hundred and twenty-five registered residents.' The woman opened her blue eyes wide and the bloke, he had the stronger pommy accent, asked me to explain as the town seemed to have far more houses than that not to count the dwellings on the claims. Made me smile that word, dwellings, but it was polite, I'll give him that. Most people would have said the miners lived in shacks. 'They ran a bit of a campaign last year to try and get more people on the electoral role so that they could get the government to increase investment in the area. Cups of tea and home-made biscuits and a spiel about the civic advantages. Reckon they must've fed the five thousand but only signed up eleven more residents.'

There was a pause. The couple exchanged glances and I answered before they could ask the question. 'I reckon there's a lot of folk want to stay under the state and federal radar.' The woman caught on pretty quick but her husband looked a bit puzzled.

'They're on the run, mate!' I told him to put him out of his misery. 'Trying to dodge the taxman, debt collectors, social services, community service and pissed off friends, grabby wives, cranky girlfriends and gobby kids. Of course some are here for the romance of the opal but that usually comes second for most of them. You only know someone here by their first name or a moniker unless they're on that electoral role.' For a minute I thought the pommy bloke looked a bit wistful and then he snapped into reality when his wife began to speak.

'Any chance you could show us how to hunt for opal? I was told that you could pick up a bit on these spoil heaps.' She was not one for hanging around. I figured that she didn't like standing. I've noticed that a bit about old women; they either want to be on the move or sit down. Her old man lifted his hat and wiped a line of sweat from his brow before resettling it. I was surprised to see that he had a thick thatch of grey hair. At least they were wearing lids that gave them a decent bit of protection from the sun and both were in long sleeves. Some of the idiots 'from the old country' don't take on how dangerous the heat can be until they're almost dead from dehydration and as red as boiled crayfish.

'All of these heaps around here are up for grabs.' I gestured at the white piles of dirt that surrounded us. They were pyramids of loose white soil and darker rocks about three or four metres high which had been carted out of the mines. 'Sure you want to have a go now? It's pretty hot at this time of the day and it'll be in the high thirties in a couple of hours.'

'We don't plan to stay for long. We will try looking for opal for a while and then have a bite of lunch in town,' said the bloke.

I smirked. I had heard that talk before, about making a moderate effort in the hunt for colour, and then watched people get the fever and keep on till they drop. 'The local Kourri have first dibs on the mullock heaps so steer clear of where they are working.' I nodded in the direction of three people turning stones and soil where the track ended. 'They've been here a while already, they noodle the most recent truck dumps for potch but it hasn't been real good so they will probably pack it in soon.'

The old woman looked worried. 'Look, there's no worries about doing a bit of noodling around this dump,' I assured her and I pointed at a mound of white sandstone opposite their vehicle. 'It's been here a while and no one is going to kick up rough if you find a bit of colour. Right, you need a dish and a big bottle of water.'

So I showed them how to pick up lumps of potch, turn it or even break it open looking for the shine of silicon and especially for colour. Washing likely pieces in a dish of water made it more likely they'd spot a bit of opal. I urged them to drink a lot out of that bottle as well.

And suddenly the conversation is at an end. The two of them started turning rocks and chipping at lumps of stone with other lumps of stone. They moved away from where I was standing and I was undecided what to do. I still had half a cup of cold ginger beer to finish. I thought about putting on some Hat Fitz and Cara; a bit of steel guitar and country blues to suit my mood. Instead I found myself on that same damn hill of white sandstone turning the stones, kicking at the piles of dirt, picking up potch and hoping for colour.

'Is this it?' The bloke sounded awed and uncertain. I scurried over to him and sure enough he is holding a sliver of black opal in his hand.

'Here, give it a bit of a wash and you can really see the colour.' I edged him away from the place where he'd picked up the potch. Out of the corner of my eye I could see quite a few interesting lumps in that square yard of dirt.

The water lifted the rainbow out of the rock and Matthew gasped. 'Hey, Jean, come and have a look.'

'Oh, Matthew! It's gorgeous!'

While the two of them cooed over the speck of opal I took a gander at the rocks near the old bloke's find. Sure enough there were a few more very promising pieces. I quickly slipped a couple of the biggest ones into my pocket, then I stepped smartly a couple of yards to the left of his find and started making a bit of a performance about fiddling about with the tailings there. The husband and wife stopped drooling over their bit of opal and dashed over to join me. They were besotted with the prospect of finding another bit of precious stone and started rummaging through the debris in the mullock heap with twice the effort and speed that they had exhibited earlier.

That old bloke actually gave me a look and took up a position real close to me. Find a bit of opal and you got territory and claim issues rocketing to the front. I raised my hands and shuffled even further away from that productive bit of the dump.

Old Jean gave him a bit of a look and the bloke shrugged and began hunting through the dirt. They kept at it another hour or so. I made a big show of chucking 'bloody useless' bits of rock away from where I am noodling. I threw three odd shaped lumps onto the place where Matthew found that opal to mark it. I fossicked for a bit longer, told them that I was going to call it a day and headed back to the shade by my ute.

As I anticipated the heat got to them and they decided to pack it in as well.

Jean and her old man walked over to their hired jeep. I followed, though not before I scuffed a mark in the track to direct me to the right place after they've left.

'Do you want a cuppa tea or a something?' Jean asked and she sounded tired. I calculated that she must be in her sixties. 'Matthew and I are parched. We appreciated your help and we'd love you to join us. I've got a packet of biscuits as well.'

Over the tea, Matthew and Jean told me that they will head back into town. I consoled them, 'You'll probably find some good opals in the jewellery shops. Lucky Pete has a good collection.' They told me they are staying at a camping site not far out of Lightning Ridge and they are looking forward to spending a couple of dollars on having a shower. 'This dust has made me greyer than I have to be,' said Jean. We talk a bit about the Artesian Basin and the drought.

'They've got a picture gallery in the old sheep shearing shed,' Matthew suddenly said. I was on my fourth biscuit. 'We've seen a few cattle on the property but no sheep.'

I was pleased that I could bring them up to speed on that thorny issue. They didn't get the joke but then I hadn't told my story at that point. 'The miners reckon a bloke who'd made a big strike deliberately brought Hudson Pear burrs up to Lightning Ridge. It's a bugger of a thing with hooked spikes a couple of centimetres long. They are big enough to puncture tyres and shoes. They say he scattered the burrs around his claim to discourage theft but then the plant spread like wildfire to the rest of the county.'

'But what's that to do with the lack of sheep?'

'The burr sticks to the wool of sheep and contaminates it. It plays merry hell with the shearing. Even if you can get a fleece off without wrecking your equipment on the burrs there's a big cost in combing them out of the wool. Not real good for the sheep either, as it can dig in and cause ulcers in their hide.'

Jean and Matthew looked pleased to have that bit of knowledge under their belt and so I didn't feel so bad about diddling them out of a bit of opal. Actually, I'd probably done them a big favour by ensuring their opal hunting unproductive. They started making their goodbyes.

'How long are staying here?' Jean asked me after she'd hoisted herself into the passenger seat.

'I'd thought I might head off today but...' I felt the weight of the rocks in my pocket and the insistent desire to go over that likely bit of the mullock heap. 'I reckon I might stick around a bit longer and see what I turn up.'

The Camping Host

A square bristle-haired woman sat behind a desk lifted on bricks to accommodate the bulge of a stomach twice the size of her breasts. She smiled a smile as bright as her purple shirt.

Anita joined the queue. There were two groups ahead of her preparing to pay their camping fees. On past experience Anita knew that it would be at least twenty minutes before she too would be drilled on camp safety in park sites and only then would she be able to deliver names, money and car registration. Anita didn't mind the wait. It gave her time to peruse the local information available on the walls and in the leaflets.

The most prominent sign, handwritten in black block capitals was about a dingo sighting and campers were urged not, underlined three times, to feed the wild dogs as nuisance dingoes would be shot. The full stop was the head of snarling dog. Anita wondered if the artist was the bearded man who hovered alertly behind his wife. She had emblazoned on her chest a large tag saying 'Call me Margaret'.

Anita had learnt at the Stargazer's campsite in Millstream National Park that such hosts, usually an older couple, were volunteers. Passionate folk, who, for several hours before dusk, took the money from campers, issued and checked passes, expounded on the safety issues and kept the facilities clean. They reported daily to a ranger, who'd recruited them. Some hosts stayed for months in return for free camping, wilderness on their doorstep and a small fuel allowance. 'It wouldn't be a bad way to spend a few weeks,' Anita mused.

She concentrated on reading about the state of the road access to Hancock and Joffrey Gorges. 'Forty-seven kilometres of dirt road, some of the sections with deep corrugations, and it is not recommended for two-wheel drives or caravans.' For a weird moment Anita thought that she had said those words aloud but then realised that her reading tallied with Margaret's voice delivering information to the first group, a woman and two children. The female, who said she was driving a front wheel, ten-year-old Ford, was disappointed when told her car was not suitable. She was obviously keen to avoid the extra one hundred kilometres involved in using the sealed roads, because quizzed the squat woman and asked her if she was sure she couldn't get through on the dirt. Hector, Anita could read his name tag once he moved closer to the recording table, confirmed the unsuitability of her car for the road in a determinedly patient voice. The woman scratched the back of her leg with the thonged foot of the other, took the leaflet (it repeated everything Margaret and Hector had already told her), sat at the table to fill in the form with her details, paid thirty dollars and herded her two silent children before her out of the reception hut.

Anita picked up a small book about local wattles. The beautiful colour plates and detailed descriptions of flower, leaf, branch and bark absorbed her. She concentrated on a couple of descriptions, trying to fix their characteristics in her mind; it would be so satisfying to recognise and identify a species, enunciating the Latin name with due gravitas and smugness, to an awestruck audience.

A foot shuffle alerted Anita to Hector's presence at the doorway. She watched him watch the blue Ford leave the dusty car park. 'I reckon there were five people in that car,' he said over his shoulder to Margaret.

'Can you believe some people,' she said and shook her jowls. 'Trying to cheat the park out of twenty dollars. What an example to teach your children! They're at Kookaburra 15.' Hector nodded and made a note in the little booklet that he took out of his shirt pocket. Anita wondered what process they would use to try and lever the extra money out of the cheaters then decided that the angst was all theirs. She put the wattle book back on the shelf and picked up a history of Karijini National Park as the second group moved to face Margaret over the desk.

An old bloke, with a patchy shave, settled into the chair. He announced that he, Mark and a true dinky-di Australian, was taking his three young French cobbers on a whistle and braces tour of the park. Anita was dragged away from reading history by the clunking use of several clichéd Australian terms in one sentence. She watched as he put a speckled soft hand, with two yellowed fingers, on the table and leaned towards Call me Margaret. Hovering Hector gave his beard a couple of strokes and moved in closer too. 'I want to be certain, bloody sure in fact, that Circular Pool, closed due to cyclone and flood damage in 1999, is now open.'

Anita looked at the huge poster on the wall describing the reconstructed access to beautiful Circular Pool, so did Margaret and Hector. Anita swallowed a giggle at the look on Call me Margaret's face and mentally applauded her control as she provided the leaflet with directions as to access and assured him that he and his companions could get there easily, though the swimming at Fern Pool was better.

Dinki-di Mark delivered a spiel to the hosts in a loud voice about just how Australian he was, which included being born in Perth, about his extensive outback experience and know-how in the event of fire or flood; all of which ensured, he assured Margaret, that he was just the type of mate the Frenchies needed. Margaret nodded but didn't comment. Anita figured hosts learnt pretty quickly that a verbal response, off subject, prolonged registration. Margaret nudged the registration book toward Dinky-di Mark again and asked again for forty dollars.

The old bloke ignored the registration document and leaned both freckled arms on the desk. 'I heard someone died here yesterday. Are you sure it is safe? How reliable are the safety measures? I want to know that it is all ridgy-didge. I have to look after my foreign mates, you know.'

Anita looked at the trio leaning against the wall to the right of the desk, all in their twenties and all with glazed eyes. Anita suspected that they spent quite a lot of time waiting for the old man. They didn't seem to register the grittiness of his question.

Margaret's smile slipped. 'He died through his own deliberate fault!'

Hovering Hector had stepped so close to Margaret his pot belly nudged the back of her chair but he couldn't stem her flood of words. 'He was told not climb the wall of Hancock Gorge three times, the idiot. Three times local people, and one of them a leader of the Rough Ride Tours, told him to get down as it was dangerous.' Anita saw Hector put his hand on Margaret's shoulder and squeeze.

'That tour operator, and maybe the Park, will be looking at some big costs.' Dinki-di Mark had leaned back in the seat and Anita saw him lick his thin lips. 'What was the guide doing letting someone climb up the walls of the gorge? He must be liable for slacking up on his responsibilities like that!'

'The idiot wasn't with the tour!' Margaret barked. 'He was showing off to his girlfriend. She was taking a picture of him skylarking on a ledge when it broke. He was twenty-three metres above the bottom of the gorge. He was just a stupid young man.'

Hector rushed into speech. 'It's a real shame. He was only nineteen and from Germany.' Anita shivered. Nineteen! She thought about her own son. What was it about nineteen-year-old men? They made up the major number of entries in *The Darwin Awards*. And here was another horrifically sad entry as a result of an ill-considered demonstration of bravado!

Dinki-di Mark had opened his wallet but he still hadn't finished. 'I hear that the girl is at death's door as the German fell on her!'

Margaret's reply was flat. 'Her injuries are not life-threatening.' She had quelled her urge to protect her beloved park from blame. She stared at Mark with a granite face, resentful of how he had led her into indiscretion. She twitched the forty dollars out of his hand and proffered a receipt. You can park at Galah 10. Yes?' Margaret looked past the old man, who was still seated, to Anita.

As Anita stood beside the desk listening to Call me Margaret rattle through the routine of cleanliness, rule of quiet after ten at night and the state of the roads, she wondered about that protective instinct that allowed a good person to sound off about the dreadful death of a boy as idiocy. Margaret loved this park so much she'd lost sight of the real human tragedy.

Anita, while standing beside the corner of the desk, filled in the form, wrote down a contact number and the car rego, showed their park passes and handed over her twenty dollars. All the while Dinki-di Mark sat stolidly in the plastic chair obviously waiting for a moment to grill Call me Margaret some more.

Hovering Hector walked over to Mark's foreign friends and began questioning them about their tour arrangements. Mark was out of that chair in a flash and began shepherding his flock through the door towards the ancient minibus in the car park.

'Bet he hasn't got the right insurance,' mused Hector as he watched them climb in the bus. 'I reckon he is running a clandestine tour operation. Wonder what he is charging those poor buggers for listening to his bullshit.'

'He's bloody bogus!' Margaret had transferred her disappointment with herself for losing her cool to Dinki-di Mark and glared at his registration form. Hector walked back to the desk and patted her hand. She took a deep breath and looked at me. 'Enjoy your time at Karijini,' she said and relocated her beautiful smile. 'Wear strong footwear when walking in the gorges. It is amazing how many people regret wearing thongs.'

Here and There

As she left the hut Anita relocated her own sympathy. These hosts had a hard time protecting their beloved national park when the flow of visitors included more than a few who were crass or careless. She turned in the doorway and smiled at Margaret and Hector. 'Thank you.'

True Believers

Eve squirmed. Her right leg ached and she bashed the seat in front of her as she tried to loosen the taut muscle. 'Sorry,' she whispered to the smudge of dark hair propped against the plastic window frame. There was no reply.

Eve sighed and shifted more carefully to try and find that elusive comfortable position. Her section of the cabin was in darkness and very quiet. She was hyper-aware that she was the only one moving and she felt a failure. Everyone else was still; they had managed to find the passivity and fortitude essential for enduring travelling in a crowd in an aeroplane. Eve could not.

The dark of the cabin suddenly felt gluey and thick. Eve tried to slow down her breathing. 'In two three and out two three; in two three and out two three,' she mentally chanted. She kept her mouth resolutely shut and forced the tinned air to pass in and out through her nose. It was embarrassing to be caught panting like a frightened dog. After several minutes of struggle Eve felt the tightness in her chest ease.

Her attention was dragged back to the ache in her legs. She had to resort to yet another series of moves to reposition her body within the tight confines of her inadequately padded shell seat. There was momentary relief as she had moved her weight to her left hip but it was short-lived. Eve was now even closer to her closest flying companion. She could smell the acrid remnants of his aftershave. 'Stop fiddling about,' she admonished herself silently and forced herself to stay in her new position.

She stared at the man wedged into the seat next to her. Once the two-hour fuss that followed take-off had ended, he had refused the consolation of food or drink and had eschewed entertainment, he had positioned himself very deliberately with shoes discarded, legs akimbo, seat belt under his beer belly, patriotic neck brace in place and his arms loosely folded once they had affixed the blindfold. And he had not moved once since.

Eve felt a huge bubble of envy lodge in her throat. How could he have access to the patience of Buddha while all her mantras couldn't stop her wriggling about like a worm? Eve hated his stillness. She hated the way the portions of his thick body had edged into her area of entitlement. She began to think that she could smell the stink of his feet.

Eve twisted and heaved herself into a sitting position. She tried again to assume the same posture as her neighbour but was only aware of hot hurting contact points and a stiff neck. How had the man in the next seat drilled his body to quietly endure? She longed to be able to be exhibit such resolve and stamina. Beyond his bulk she could make out all the other motionless humps of people coping admirably with being locked in a cigar box thirty-six thousand feet above the ground.

The constant drone of the engines was louder since the last wailing child had been lulled or drugged into sleep. She felt them thrum in her ear and vibrate her body; it was like being in an unpleasant embrace. She looked at her watch. Less than ten minutes since she had last looked.

Eve shuddered. Her thoughts flickered between the points of pain where her body was pressed into the seat; the awful pressure on her ears; and the suffocating constriction of the belt, which she dared not remove, gripping her waist.

She could not even seek the solace of the back of the seat entertainment as the flickering blue light was likely to induce the nausea that she had taken pills to restrain. She wished that she had insisted on being given sleeping pills too.

'Just toss back a few more drugs to make it better,' she raged at herself. She was overwhelmed by a sickening realisation that everyone else on the plane was much better suited to dealing with difficulties whereas she, Eve, indulged herself in the discomforts that pressed upon her.

How the minutes to the end of this awful imprisonment crawled!

Eve felt her stomach roil. Sitting for hours was bad for the back and the gut. She contemplated getting out of her seat and heading for the plastic cubicle at the back of the plane but decided that she was not sufficiently uncomfortable. Eve feared to undo her belt.

Eve felt a profound sense of despair she did not have the fortitude, the endurance and the patience of her fellow travellers. They had resigned themselves to the rigors of being shut up in a thin-skinned plane and therefore found rest. They were reconciled to being supported in thin air by the ear bashing thrum of four massive engines and so they were at ease. They were soothed and confident in the abilities and good intentions of the pilot and crew. They had accepted the inconveniences for the great benefits of speedy travel and they slept contentedly in its embrace.

Eve did not share in this confidence.

She was afraid because her lack of confidence in the competency of the plane, its engines and its crew was growing. She was suddenly afraid her agitations would affect the performance of the plane. She squinted at the shadowy statues of human lumps through the gloom. She froze in her seat as the realisation hit her that it was their quiet prostration that was keeping the plane afloat. She was stunned. No wonder everyone was so quiet. They were praying.

Here and There

Eve felt the plane plunge. She lifted a few centimetres out of her seat but the belt grabbed and dragged her back. The plane steadied. The warning lights flashed and the captain's smooth voice assured them that the turbulence would not last long and instructed passengers to remain seated. Several lights flicked on in the cabin but most of the passengers were still and faithful.

There were several more ups and downs, though none as significant as that first buffet. Eve knew she had to repudiate her doubts. She knew that she was causing the plane to buck and heave in the air. Eve could not find the faith. She didn't have enough belief to keep them airborne; she knew they were going to crash. She was panting and did not know how to stop.

She was making the plane crash because she did not believe.

She began to cry. She unclipped her seat belt. Eve realised the only answer was to get off the plane; the plane wanted her and her damaging doubts ejected.

The man next to her clasped her hand. 'It'll be over in a few moments.' His voice was low and homely. 'Just wait a little and it'll all be good. Smooth as silk just like it was before.'

Eve trembled and held tight to the calloused hand with both of hers. She sat very, very still though her heart hammered and her breath fluttered. 'There's always a bit of weather around this part of the trip.' His Australian drawl was familiar and comforting. 'Nothing to worry about.' Eve decided that he sounded like her father.

The captain assured them that the worst was over, she would switch off the seat belt signs and passengers could once again move about the cabin. Eve still gripped her neighbour's hand but not as grimly. He turned a bit more in his seat so he could pat her hands with his big left paw. 'See, it's steady now. Nice and steady. You don't have to worry any more cos we're all right.'

W Lodwick Lowdon

Rubbish

Ann and Carl cycled along the white towpath to Hungerford. They had moored their narrow boat by Froxfield Lower Lock and were combining a tour of the village with a reconnaissance of where they could moor overnight. Not many boats were on the move so they were optimistic about securing a reasonable situation.

Scarcely a mile from where they had temporarily moored they could see an old red bridge which arched over the green water of the canal and framed the pleasant country scene beyond. The water rippled in the wake of a convoy of ducks. 'A sweet, especial rural scene!' Carl shouted the quote at his wife's back. The bridge had a second span to the right of the towpath which allowed the road to travel over the River Dan as well as the canal. The pretty shallow river was three or four yards lower than canal to which it flowed parallel.

The water was so clear Ann could easily see the yellow and white stones on the river bottom and the fronds of green cress that waved their fringes in the water. At the bridge she crouched low over her bike to make it under its slanted wall and suddenly wobbled to a stop; Carl had to press hard on his brake handles so he didn't run into her. 'Carl! It's disgusting!'

The towpath and slope down to the river side were studded with busted shopping bags. A fly-tipper had tossed heaps of rubbish off the bridge. Ann and Carl had to dismount and wheel their bikes around the couple of plastic humps that had disgorged their smelly, lurid coloured contents over the path and many more had tumbled down the river side. 'What a mess.' Carl's expression was as sour as the smell from the rubbish.

On their return journey a couple of hours later they were unsurprised but disappointed to find the rubbish still strewn about; however, Ann and Carl were prepared. Ann propped her bike against the bridge side and dug yellow plastic gloves and a roll of heavy duty black bags out of the pannier. 'Sure you want to do the pick up?' he asked again. Ann just nodded. Carl gave her a wave and cycled off to fetch the boat. He would pick up his wife, her bike and the bags of rubbish and then they would carry onto Hungerford. They had located a Canal Trust rubbish point and they had decided to use the boat to carry the bags away from the watercourses. It was beyond Hungerford, at Kintbury, which did mean having the rubbish on board overnight. 'I know it is not ideal,' Ann had coaxed her husband into agreement, 'but needs must. We can't just leave it there.'

Ann had picked up rubbish in public places before. She would mutter crossly as she stuffed bits of plastic or tin in her old coat. Once or twice she had gone to her car for a carrier bag to clear an area. Never had she seen a dump so blatant. 'What were they thinking?' Ann wondered. She opened one of the bags and began filling it with rubbish. She was mindful of Carl's warnings about injury and used sticks to shove soft items into the black bag.

The rubbish, which so offended and annoyed her, soon also began to make Ann very sad. So many of the items spewing out of the bags were good clothes in bright sporting colours, they had been tainted by contents of juice cartons, fast food remnants, teabags and coffee grains. 'Why didn't they take the clothes to a charity shop or something?' she asked the air. A pair of denim jeans, artfully frayed, with a diamanté belt made her pause. They had been stuffed into one of the broken shopping bags with a dirty nappy, an empty tin of baked beans and a sodden tea towel that followed. 'This doesn't make sense!'

Ann squashed her questions and her pauses. All she wanted was to get this nasty job over and done with so she concentrated on tossing items into a second and a third bin bag as fast as she could.

She found a child's tweed jacket. She laid it gently on the grass. More children's clothes spilled out of the ripped Littlewoods' bag. There was even a bright red Mickey Mouse scarf with matching hat; they looked like they had never been worn. But these clothes had also been shoved in with more kitchen rubbish and another dirty nappy and they could not be salvaged.

Ann stopped. She felt rather sick because she was sure that these were gifts; presents that had been wasted in this very disrespectful way.

She looked at the remaining ripped and overfull dumped bags that spilled their contents down the slope to the river. Ann would have to scrabble through a wooden fence with her black roll of rubbish bags to get to them. While Ann dithered Carl had drawn the boat up beside her and called to her to take the rope. As soon as the boat had nestled into the side of the canal he stepped onto the towpath and began hammering in pins. 'Carl, do you think I should separate the good and the bad rubbish?'

'What?'

'Those bags on the riverbank look to be mainly made up of shoes. 'I wonder if I should be recycling some of the items. It seems so wasteful to simply put them in a skip.'

'Just stuff it in a bag. Stop making a palaver of it and let's just get it done.'

Carl and Ann clambered through the wooden fence and Carl shook out a bag and held it for Ann to throw the rubbish into. 'Look at all these shoes, there must be ten or twelve pairs! Why are all these shoes being dumped? Why were these decent and pretty things being thrown away?' Carl just shook the bag impatiently. Ann felt very uncomfortable as if she, by pushing someone's belongings into the rubbish bag, was helping whoever intended to hurt that someone by dumping their stuff. Ann felt wounded and dirty just by being a witness to how far one person was prepared to go to punish another.

As she transferred the shoes to the bigger stronger bags Carl held for her, Ann realised that each shoe was damaged so it was unwearable. One pair of high heels, covered in diamantes to match the belt she had seen earlier, had the ankle straps cut. The leather on the boots had been gouged. This act of fly tipping oozed maliciousness.

In the last pile of rubbish clothes and shoes were again interspersed with food scraps. But there was a nastier development: make-up and powder had been upended and a large bottle of moisturizing lotion had been squirted onto the clothes. The spite made Ann's hands shake and she transferred the soiled clothes into the hardy bin bag Carl was holding as fast as she could.

'You can't dump rubbish here!' someone bellowed in her ear from the bridge. Ann leapt in fright.

Carl was quick to take umbrage. 'We're picking it up!' he shouted right back and 'You stupid gits,' hung in the air. Ann and Carl started ferrying the bags up the slope to the towpath.

'We're taking it to Kintbury to get rid of it,' she explained. 'We didn't want it to foul the water.'

He and she, locals and regular towpath walkers, had come down the steps to the towpath and were now as quick with their thanks and praise as they had been with their blame. Once all nine bin bags were transferred from the towpath and piled on the front deck and Ann's bike lifted onto the roof, Carl pulled up the mooring pins. He pushed the front of the narrow boat towards the centre of the canal before he jumped on the back. The locals waved but Carl didn't wave back. He was cross. 'Lots of words but they didn't help to put the bags onto the boat.'

'Perhaps it was because they didn't have yellow gloves,' Ann said. She knew he would be grumpy until they could dump the rubbish bags. He hated seeing his dear narrow boat bulging with pollution. Ann was even more anxious to get rid of the reeking things.

Here and There

It'll Be Grand

The wife really rated that grand piano. It had the right name and a provenance. Sure it had been out of tune for several years but it had gravitas, literally.

She gets sentimental about things, my wife. Gives a thing a spirit or yearning; then that thing says it is mostly yearning to be with her. True enough once that thing had wheedled its way into our house, because she has an arm lock on my heart, the what-have-you gets maximum attention; the wood glows with polish, the leather with cream and the china gleams.

Now, this grand piano told her how it required a caring home and how it would enhance the musical genius of our daughter. 'It is essential,' said my wife, her dyed red hair crackling with energy, 'not only for the development of her music but for the thorough and complete enjoyment of the music.' She had already cleared a space, cleared a room in fact, in anticipation of its arrival. 'After all,' she reassured me, 'it's only a baby grand piano.'

My wife had visited this piano, which lived just over fifty miles from our home, while I had been on a job in Birmingham. She had taken the Volkswagen Golf GTI and made a reconnaissance. That piano lived in a house on a hill outside a country town. The distance from the main centres explained the relatively modest cost of the huge piece of kit. The owners were desperate to reclaim a room in their house, which had enabled the further discount the wife was able to wrangle and another couple of hundred knocked off because she had arranged that I would pick it up the next day.

Here and There

'Pick it up!' said I to the wife. 'What with, a crane?' But then she tells me that she called in a couple of favours from the Wright boys and they are going to provide the low-loader, a bit of muscle and the rugs and strapping for the trip back home. Very pleased about the low-loader, was the wife, as it would ensure that the main street and the other roads near our house would be made aware of our cultural acquisition.

'Oh, Johnnie,' and she stroked my shoulders and kissed me plumb on the mouth, 'it's only a baby. Though I admit it's on the bigger scale,' she chuckled.

I did wonder if three men, however hearty, would be enough to manhandle a grand piano onto the truck. I did a bit of research in the evening before I jumped in the cab with the Wrights. At six-foot-six we were looking at a beast of an instrument of polished rosewood weighing in at almost eight hundred pounds. It was no baby! I admit I was pretty impressed with the price the wife had negotiated for the Bluthner 1901. I rang the local music shop and got Paul Drake's take on the manpower required. He tells me that it may be too big for the dolly, which he'll lend me for a token amount, because it's only good on the flat. He recommended getting in a professional team but we were moving into expensive territory there so I just grunted and hung up. I did realise that I had better rustle up another couple of mates and lay in a few more beers for the celebration when we get back.

I enjoyed the drive with Dwayne and Laurie. I caught up on a bit of gossip, heard about some jobs in the offing and added a couple of tales to my repertoire. Mick and Adam were in their white van and followed along behind. We wasted a bit of time identifying the correct house disguised as by similar-looking yew hedges. Also, the wife didn't warn us the driveway was on the long and narrow side. We had to park up on the road and check it out which involved a hike up to the house. There was enough turning at the top so long as the piano owner moved his vehicle out of the way. He was so pleased to see us that he was in that Volvo like shot and parked her out behind Mick's van. Dwayne slowly reversed the flatbed up the driveway to the house.

It was a nice place. 'Built in the fifties,' my new mate Jeff told me. The driveway looped around the hillock on which the house was perched. I could see lots of big windows and a stone patio graced the front of the house. A massive bronze fish was fountaining water into the air on the right-hand side of the house. 'That's a big pond,' I observed and Jeff agreed it was.

It was also in a hell of a place to get a piano out of. Jeff had told the wife, which she had neglected to tell me, that the piano could only go out the patio doors and not through the house. Pretty obvious when you stood there and looked at it. However, the pond, a bloody big stretch of lilies with a wooden Japanese bridge, blocked the passage that the piano had taken into the house some thirty years earlier. 'I wish I'd brought the crane,' I groaned. Jeff agreed it might have been helpful.

'We'll have to manoeuvre her down the slope to the driveway,' was Mick's opinion and in the end we all had to agree it was the only way. Dwayne drove the flatbed to the point below where we would come off the grass with the piano. We wrapped the piano in sacking to protect it from the straps we were going to use to ease her down the slope on the dolly. The Wrights took the straps and stood a bit back and to the right and left. Mick and Adam were hands on, lifting at the corners, and I was volunteered to take the downhill position for the lift. The plan was that Jeff, who said he had a poorly knee, would give directions as I shuffled backwards. A grand, especially this baby, was not just heavy it was awkward. I failed to feel anything but animosity for the wife and her pet piano as I edged slowly down the grassy hillock. Jeff kept up a cheerful chatter of encouragement. I regretted the inadequate tread on my boots though I reckoned bloody crampons would have been the right call.

We were about three quarters of the way down the slope when my downhill leg began to slide and I lost contact with the piano. I could feel myself moving into the splits as my uphill leg was trapped under the descending piano. I bellowed a bit as the groin pain intensified. I screamed a little because I could not get my head out of way of a piano fast edging towards me. I lurched backward, still in a limbo splits position, but only made a few inches. The Wright brothers hauled on the straps, the men at the sides threw their weight onto the piano and the dolly gouged a couple of trenches in the grass. They stopped the descent just as my eyelashes brushed against the varnish. I admit I whimpered a bit but, under the eyes of the other men, I pulled myself together and took another grip.

'Jeez, we were lucky to get her down in one piece,' says Jeff. I stared at him in astonishment. '*We* had successfully pushed the piano up the boards onto the flatbed and tied it down. The real muscle were having a laugh and drinking the mugs of weak tea provided by the lady of the house.

'It was a bit hairy there for a bit,' Jeff went on. 'I wasn't sure we'd hold her especially as I'd watered the grass last night and you know what it's like, slippery when wet!'

Edith Williams

Edith Williams was enjoying a cup of coffee and a slice of superb chocolate cake seated at the window table in Annabelle's Coffee House. At least two thirds of the other tables were occupied by students from the nearby college. Edith enjoyed the snippets of banter that lifted out of the masses of hair arched over mobiles; it reminded her of what she was missing and, as a shrill, mean laugh hit the ceiling, what she was not.

Edith was sure that Annabelle had not intended that the majority of her clientele be sixth form students, they were hard on the furniture and the crockery. She had obviously adapted, as the menu was more subway and pop than tea, scones and cream, but the quality of her cakes indicated Annabelle's own preferences and drew Edith to return regularly. Next time, she told herself, she would make sure she avoided the lunch hour.

The door of the café opened.

A tall woman stood on the step gripping the handle. She made no move to come in. Her hungry eyes skipped and skittered over the gathering. She was panting.

The students' indolent sprawls were replaced by straight backs and wary eyes. A message pinged for attention and was ignored.

'Where's Bethany?' the woman at the door gasped. 'You must know. You have to tell me.'

No-one answered. Some were staring at the table and others were carefully, quietly scooping items into their bags. The smell of a hot chocolate drink on the service counter was thick and cloying. The smell drifting in from the woman in the doorway was mousy and stale.

'It's been three weeks now. You're her friends. You'd know where she'd go. She'd tell you and you have to tell me,' the woman's voice could be easily heard in the silent café.

The café continued to sit in silence. Almost thirty people under the age of twenty and not a sound. Edith Williams was in awe; not even exams had commanded such a silence.

Annabelle, lean and florally aproned, came into the café from the kitchen. 'Mrs Watkins,' she almost whispered, 'Bethany isn't here. I haven't seen her for weeks. None of us have.'

The woman remained in the doorway. Her unevenly buttoned coat flexed in the breeze. From her window position Edith Williams could see students, who had wished to enter the café, take one look at blockage in the door, about face and scatter.

'But where is Bethany?' the woman's voice ached with desperation. Edith Williams realised how gaunt the woman was under her badly fitting clothes.

Annabelle advanced towards Mrs Watkins and made sweeping movements with her hands. 'You have to go now! As you can see Bethany is not here!'

'Bethany's not here.' Her mother repeated the words in a tired, tired voice.

'Go and see Mr Pritchard at the school,' Annabelle said.

'They won't let me. I'm a nuisance and I upset the children.' Mrs Watkins showed her grey teeth.

Annabelle took heart from the idea that other organisations had driven this demented woman from their door. 'Mrs Watkins, Bethany is not here. You have to go.' The woman continued to stand in the doorway. 'She's probably at home,' said Annabelle in a burst of cruel invention. 'You had better go home and check.'

Mrs Watkins turned in a flurry of new purpose and reeled away down the street.

Annabelle shut the door. 'There now,' she said loudly to the still silent youths, 'she's gone home and she won't be disturbing us again.' She looked at Edith Williams and said, 'Poor lady, poor lady. It is so very upsetting. Jasmin!' The waitress so addressed jumped as if she'd been pricked. 'See if anyone wants a nice drink or a bit of cake before they go back to classes.'

The last sentence had the opposite effect to what she had intended. As if released from a spell the young people abandoned seats and surged out of the door of the café. Several of the plates had sandwiches that had scarcely been touched and glasses were left half empty. 'Must be bad to go off their food,' muttered Edith Williams, and then privately admonished herself for being so flippant about a tragic situation.

Annabelle twisted her apron in her hands, unwittingly creating abstract effects with the cloth as she watched her customers desert the shop. Edith Williams saw the three waitresses, who were of an age with the fleeing throng, were about to follow them out the door. Annabelle interrupted their flight and began chivvying them to clear the tables.

She leaned against the door now herself. 'Third time in a fortnight!' Annabelle was talking at Edith Williams. 'Do you want another tea? I'll share it with you. I am desperate for a sit down.' Desperate to talk was how Edith Williams understood the offer and she gestured to the opposite side of the table. 'She's killing business, you know. Janice at the Nest is having uncomfortable visits as well. The students do a runner when they see her coming. It'll be days before they work up any enthusiasm to leave the campus and come here again; especially now that they know she is banned from the college.'

No tea was ordered or delivered to the table but Edith Williams sat quietly.

'I don't know how long this will take to blow over. She was an awkward girl when she came to the café.' Edith Williams raised an eyebrow. 'Bethany, she was intense with the other students. She was not a relaxed or comfortable person. She was a red girl – red hair and orange freckles. Sometimes bright and bossy and then surly and silent. And now that she has run away she has created even more awkwardness and tension. That poor woman!' And Edith Williams knew that the soliloquy had now flicked to Mrs Watkins. 'She prowls around the town day after day looking and asking about the girl. How could she just run off and leave her mother in such a state? I don't know whether to persevere with the students or aim at the oldies.' It took a moment for Edith to follow Annabelle's skip from tragedy to the prosaic matter of business. 'The young have all the money these days. I wish that stupid girl would let someone know that she is safe so we could get some peace.'

Annabelle rose to her feet. 'I don't know what I am going to do. 'Karen, sweep the floor and then, if it is tidy in the kitchen, you, Jasmin and Ellen may as well go. I don't expect there will be much business for the rest of the afternoon.' The waitresses sped around the café. The prospect of an early finish made them brisk and efficient. Within ten minutes they had on coats and were scurrying out of the café.

Edith Williams was not sure what made her follow them. She had a nose for trouble and the troubled. Apart from the three young women in front of her there was no-one on the street. It was as if Mrs Watkin's dreadful grief had blighted the whole town.

The three girls went straight into a pub, the Loggerheads. It was an old building, with plastic bunting and a blackboard advertising a live band on Friday nights. Its white walls were dull, the windows smudged and the footpath outside was littered with cigarette butts. Another establishment that catered for students, who cared only to focus on each other and paid little heed to the attractiveness, or not, of the places where they spent their time.

Edith Williams paused for a couple of minutes and then went into the pub herself.

Once inside the interior of the pub it took a couple of moments for Edith William's eyes to adjust to the darkness after the brightness of the autumn sunlight. She spied the girls in a corner of the lounge with hands wrapped around Cokes liberally spiked with, Edith Williams guessed, rum or vodka. She dithered and then headed for the ladies. In the bold neon of the-better-than-she-expected toilet facilities she asked herself what on earth she was doing tracking these young women.

Edith Williams left the toilets with the definite intention of quietly slipping out of the door but the sight of one of the girls already back at the bar and ordering another round of double rum and Cokes made her change her mind. She walked over to the bar, ordered herself a ginger beer, took a deep breath and marched over to the corner table and sat down with the three waitresses, who'd already taken huge swallows of their second round of drinks. By strategically placing her large handbag on the floor to the right and angling the chair to the left she effectively slowed down any attempt at escape.

'She's dead, isn't she!' Edith Williams declared matter factually to the girls.

Ellen burst into tears. 'Yes, she's dead. She's dead. Yes, she is.' The last affirmation was almost a shout.

Jasmine and Karen were pinned to their seats by panic.

'How did she die?' All the girls shook their heads, not so much in denial as in horror. 'Tell me.' Edith Williams put all forty years of teaching authority into her voice and the loom of her body. 'Tell me how!'

'At the party,' Jasmine whispered. Edith Williams kept up the pressure with her posture and a neutral expression.

'In the quarry,' Karen quavered. 'It's got good acoustics,' she added irrelevantly. 'Ken had driven his car there and he has a real good sound system.'

Ellen was still sobbing. Karen continued, 'We'd taken a couple of bottles. Everybody brought something.'

'Everybody?' Edith Williams echoed.

'There were about sixty of us. It was like a picnic. Sort of an end of summer event before college got on top of us. You know exams and stuff,' Karen answered.

'Bethany came,' blurted Ellen. 'We couldn't get rid of her.'

'We knew she wouldn't like it!'

'She was desperate to come. She had a thing for Henry.' Ellen started crying again.

'He hated her!' declared Karen. 'Called her names. You know, minging.'

He made her feel bad but she sort of kept hanging around.' Jasmine shook her hair. 'She kept, like, kept after him. She was all mushy and clinging and silly about him.'

Edith Williams nodded. The desperate need to tell and the effects of the rum and Cokes had the story flowing out of their mouths.

'Told her not to come,' declared Karen. 'She turned up anyway. She was covered in make-up and she was wearing a really short dress. I told her it wasn't going to work.'

'Henry had been drinking before he got to the party,' Ellen declared. 'Everyone was drinking and dancing. It was like a bit wild when Bethany got there. Johnny was already being sick in the bushes.'

'I went off with Jasmine and the Crow twins, you know.'

Ellen began to sob again.

'Sit up and tell me,' Edith Williams instructed the melting girl. 'Go on.'

Ellen hiccoughed. 'Bethany and I were dancing. I love dancing and Bethany does too.' There was a dreadful gasp and Jasmine put her trembling hands under the table. 'Then there was a sort of break in the music. She went looking for Henry and he was with Alan. Alan deals, you know. He brings the E and the grass and stuff.' Her voice was getting very small. 'Bethany got all uptight.'

'When we got there,' Jasmine picked up the story, 'she was shouting. She was saying about the dangers of drugs, sort of like in the classroom.'

'She was saving Henry,' said Karen.

'She said she would tell!'

'Henry and Alan were really mad.'

'Really mad! Everyone was mad. And there was lots of shouting.'

The words were pouring out of the girls. They tumbled over each other to tell the story.

'Alan grabbed her and sort of pushed her down. Her dress got ripped and her face got all smeared. She looked pretty off.'

'It was ugly!' Edith Williams was not sure if they were speaking about Bethany or the actions of the drunk young men.

'While Alan held her down.'

'He was sitting on her belly while she was wriggling her legs.'

'Henry sort of shoved tablets in her mouth. Mandy, Alan's girlfriend—'

'Slave you mean!'

'Poured beer into her mouth.'

'It was pretty ugly.'

'All the time Henry was shouting about how she couldn't tell now, could she. Other people were shouting yeah, she couldn't tell now,' Ellen's voice was choked with snot and tears.

'And then she sort of stopped kicking,' Jasmine said in a thin whisper.

Edith Williams repressed her horror at the use of 'sort of'.

'Just stopped,' echoed Karen.

And the three girls stopped.

Edith Williams sighed. The girls had slumped. Their faces were variations in grief and horror. In the flickering light of the pub it was as if their anguish was set in stone. Edith Williams sighed again.

'Bethany must be restored to her mother,' she said to Jasmine, Ellen and Karen. 'She must now be treated with dignity and given a proper burial. She deserves your justice and friendship.'

All three girls jerked at the last words. Jasmine was trembling and had her hands wrapped in her thin jumper, stretching the fabric down so that the lacy bra showed. Karen had turned a dreadful yellow and Edith Williams wondered if she might faint. Ellen was still crying, three rising breaths to a squeak with each sob; her eyes were almost buried in the swollen flesh. Edith Williams saw that the cheap mascara had made dark blotches on her cheeks and chin. Like Bethany.

'We will go to the college. We begin with Mr Underwood and then the rest will unfold as it should.'

W Lodwick Lowdon

Growing at Home

Isabelle, her friend from school, had taken early retirement from her significant role in the bank; choosing to leave on a high with a gong and an excellent retirement package. She knew Bernice had been three years a widow, after nursing her husband through a long illness, and knew too she had not returned to her job with the council.

Izzie had rung in February and enthused to Bernie about her plan, part of her bucket list, to visit all the important gardens in England. She was sure that Bernie would be just the most appropriate companion for regular mid-week jaunts especially as she was already a long-time member of the National Trust.

'It'll be fun, Bernie dear, and it will give you a chance to make use of that card of yours.'

Bernice expressed a little surprise about the plan as the single visit she had made to Isabelle's house had not encouraged her to think that Isabelle liked gardening. The front of her house had been covered in heavy pebbles, like those found on a Norfolk shingle, on which were perched too-heavy-to-steal bronze ceramic pots filled with different coloured grasses. The larger piece of land at the back was Japanese in tone, and featured paths and granite seats and twisted lumps of wood and unusual conifers.

Isabelle declared that her love of gardening had been restricted by her devotion to work and the theatre but she wished to rectify the matter and learn all about it. 'Bernie, my dear friend, you are the best person to go to gardens with. You have such love of plants and gardens, and that makes you the perfect person with whom to embark upon my mission.'

Bernice was not sure about the hyperbole concerning her relationship with plants. 'Well I do enjoy my garden. There are some exotic exceptions but it is in the main a cottage garden.' Bernice could feel herself weakening in the face of tactics Izzie had very effectively used of old.

She quickly expressed some trepidation about the plan in terms of travel. 'But how will I get there, Izzy?' She found that Isabelle had thought that one through as well. She explained that, given the placement of Bernie's home, a small house in a cul-de-sac less than two miles from the train station in Warwick, she could take the train to the nearest station of the agreed upon garden. 'I,' said Isabelle, who lived in Beaconsfield, 'will motor to that station and pick you up.'

They had to wait until the last weeks of March, after Bernice was persuaded by Isabelle's bright blandishments, for gardens to open to visitors. This gave Bernice the opportunity to gracefully resign from the committee of the local WI which met on the day that Isabelle had decided was most suitable for their regular meetings. It also gave her time to peruse the neat little book provided annually by the National Trust and make her garden selections. The book was unforthcoming concerning nearby railway stations. The NT definitely favoured the car, but Bernice made good use of the information provided by the internet as to train timetables.

For several months, week after week, the two women visited the great gardens of England. They arrived as close to opening time as possible. Isabelle relished powering her royal green MG, also a consequence of the bucket list, through the gates of their chosen destination. Bernice held onto her hat and laughed at Izzie's motoring swagger.

Isabelle was methodical about preparing for each visit. She always came armed with a synopsis of a suitable analysis of each garden. She was informed about all the names of garden designers; she was engaged by the grand concept and critical of its delivery. She was impatient with any indication that season should be permitted to interfere in the delivery of the garden's impact. 'Drama,' she pronounced, 'could and should be attained, regardless of the flowers, by the use of effective use of stone, concrete and evergreen features.'

Isabelle kept notes of each visit in which she graded the gardens by a star system, took scenic pictures from high points and wrote pithy comments about the beds, parks and orchards. She checked the garden of now against its original plan. These notes were the basis of Isabelle's carefully worded weekly blog entitled, 'Travels through the Great Gardens of England'.

Bernice liked to let the garden speak to her before she considered other visitors' interpretations. She trailed in Isabelle's wake because she was continually being captured by a plant of unusual foliage or exotic bloom. On most trips she lost Izzy when she paused to revel in the beauty of an established tree. Bernice appreciated the hours that kept the beds tidy and swooned over the lavish planting of more common flowers. She stroked the bark of trees, lifted blooms and peered into their depths, dandled a hand in lily-clad ponds and wallowed in the rich scents of each garden. She rarely proceeded down a path in a straight line.

Isabelle said, in the third month, impatient with her dawdling, 'Your focus is on the minutia because you're so short-sighted, Bernie.' Bernice mentally quarrelled with the 'so' but accepted the rebuke, picked up her pace and tried to look at the breadth, length and impact of the garden as a whole. It was a revelation to take the long view. Bernice began to see not only individual plants but the architecture of the gardens. By mid-summer she entered into lively debates with Isabelle about style, effect, accommodating plants getting bigger and the resultant changes in light over quiche and salad. Isabelle gave grades for taste and presentation concerning their lunches in her blog as well.

Isabelle visited Bernice's home once that year. It was late summer and Isabelle announced she would pick Bernie up from her home in Warwick because the garden that they had determined to visit was close in Baddesley Clinton. In anticipation of Izzy's visit, Bernice had spent several extra hours in her garden removing weeds and straightening edges. Isabelle refused coffee so she could spend a few moments being guided around 'the policies'. She liked the brook at the end of the back garden and nodded with enthusiasm when Bernie described the carpet of primroses and bluebells in spring. She admired the small orchard and sympathised about the necessary reduction of the vegetable plot. She described the flower beds that filled the front garden as quaint. 'It is so very, very much a Bernie creation!' Izzy hugged her friend a quick hug and led the way to the car.

Bernice struggled through that day. The glories of this grand garden seemed only to highlight the inadequacies of her little patch. She found the lunch dry and tasteless although Isabelle gave it a four-star ranking. Bernice was immensely relieved when the day was over and she was dropped off on the forecourt of her house. 'I won't stay. If I buzz off immediately I will beat the traffic.' Bernice did not persist with her invitation but she stayed on the pavement waving goodbye until Isabelle had driven away with a cheerful tootle from the horn of her MG.

As soon as the MG was out of sight Bernice turned to look at her garden. She was instantly and uncomfortably aware that her garden was a hotchpotch of straggling shrubs and summer flowers which jockeyed with a random planting of roses for space and light. There was a multitude of colours but, looking at it with a critical eye, it was more like the messy palette of an artist rather than of a picture.

For several days Bernice moped. She would gaze at her garden through the front bay window and sigh. She would return from grocery shopping, pause by the front gate and groan. She would hang her clothes on the line and keep her eyes on the pegs. The green bank, on which Bernice had expended very little attention once she had dug in the hundreds of bulbs years ago, seemed smug and detached. Indeed, Bernice felt almost a horror of going into her garden because she was assailed by her lack of artistic vision.

It was a magazine in the dentist's waiting room that restored Bernice to herself and to her garden. The picture showed a room paved in yellow and white squares; heavy yellow brocade curtains hung about a huge window that looked onto flat green fields. She tore the picture out, folded it into her bag ignoring the murmurings of disapproval.

She stood motionless for long, long minutes before her garden but this time she wasn't looking for the flaws but at the possibilities. Finally she clapped her hands together and darted inside for drawing paper but she could only find some rather sad lined foolscap. Bernice drew a breath and ordered herself to slow down. 'Tea first,' she announced to Adam's photograph.

Eased into a quieter state of mind by the act of making tea and the longer act of drinking it, Bernice realised that she had blank paper in the photocopier and there was a clip board. Armed, she went outside immediately, determined record the size and colour of the plants in her front garden. It took her several hours over a few days, much longer than she anticipated. She struggled to recall the position and colour of some of her spring flowering plants because Bernice had decided to make her front garden yellow and white, just yellow and white, simply yellow and white.

Her diagrams indicated that she would have to move about thirty plants before winter. The blue ceanothus was huge but Bernice was determined to prune it and shift it; lupins and delphiniums were on the relocation list as well. Her main concern was the roses. There were ten, only one of which was yellow. They had been in her garden a long time; she and Adam had planted most of them shortly after they moved in fifteen years ago. She was anxious that they would be damaged but she was determined: move they must.

Bernice felt empowered by her prospective ruthlessness. She particularly looked forward to removing the lamia with its vulgar pink flower tower and the limp lobelia. The heather was old and woody and it probably needed a good burning years ago. The berberis darwinii with its spiky leaves and bright orange flowers would be put beside the garage. Bernice was thrilled with her vision.

Isabelle rang in February. She was recently returned from a month in Florida, one more to cross off the bucket list, and she had another proposal for Bernie. Yes, she knew they had only visited a small number of the gardens on offer, none of those in Cornwall or Norfolk, but she implored Bernie, 'This year would you explore the Border castles with me?' She informed Bernie that she had a blog readership of more fifteen hundred and she believed that they had an appetite for 'ye olde stone'.

Bernice had laughed. Isabelle certainly knew how to rev up Bernice's life but she wasn't adverse to more action. 'It's a great idea, Izzy.' She told Isabelle that she felt that they should make their visits to stone fortresses fortnightly and suggested they stay overnight at local pubs or B & Bs. 'All the more ballast for the blog, Izzy.' Isabelle had cooed with delight.

'Let's begin with Whittington and Chirk in late March,' Izzy declared.

Throughout the reorganisation of her front garden Bernice had shied away from the issue of the cherry tree. It was an old and beautifully shaped tree that every year was covered with hundreds of pink blossoms that held their perfection for barely two weeks and then rained faded petals on the plants and shrubs beneath. Bernice loved the tree. As the snowdrops and primroses gave way to the daffodils and the narcissi she saw the cherry begin to bud. The drama of the yellow and white was crisp and fascinating. How would the cherry fit into this designed garden? How would the sunrise pink fare against a picture in white and gold? Bernice prepared to harden her heart. She prepared explanatory speeches to the shade of Adam who had loved the tree. She prepared justifications for the neighbours and even a letter to the paper about choice and change.

When the tree bloomed no choice was necessary. The tree, enriched by the addition of several bags of compost and lavished with water, shone with blossom and buzzed with bees. The contrast between the cherry and the white and yellow plants nestled under it was magnificent.

Discretion

Denise staggered down the steps of the bus. The three bulging plastic bags gripped in her left hand swung heavily against her legs as she lurched to the ground. The smoked mackerel package gouged a hole in her tights and the cheapest tin of tomatoes smashed a bruise into her calf.

Denise cursed Wednesday as she always did because Wednesday was shopping day. The day she went straight from her work as the dentist's receptionist to the supermarket.

It had been, as she expected, a dire experience. Brash lighting emphasised the garish colours of the packaging to the point that anything orange seemed luminescent. The place was awash with noise: rasping air-conditioning, screeching carts carrying shrieking kids, shopping lists debated on mobiles and the constant trill of talking tills telling you to put your items in the bag. Denise had chosen a human to bleep her shopping. She had peered at the nametag and wished Danny a good day. That and her other cheery comments had had only grunts in response. 'May as well have gone to the talking till,' Denise had commented impatiently to Danny as she had paid cash for her food. Her rudeness had haunted her throughout the bus ride.

From the bus stop it was more than a half mile to the busy bridge over the canal. The bags were particularly heavy this week; the cans were the real drag on the arms. The previous week's haul of toilet paper and kitchen towel had also been awkward but that had been bulk not weight. Denise regretted the impulse buy of a cheap bottle of Australian Chardonnay but the price had seduced her.

As soon as she set foot on the towpath Denise's spirits rose. *Heron's Egg* was only two hundred yards from the bridge; a lucky break to have found such a convenient mooring for the spring and summer. The canal bent in a long curve and Denise's small narrow boat nestled against the bank out of sight from the road. When she was within a few feet of the boat Denise paused to appreciate her colours, grey and blue, and the dark flight of the heron to her nest painted on her bow. The clean windows reflected the evening light and shone yellow. It was as if *Heron' Egg* was signalling a welcome aboard. Denise loved her narrow boat with passion.

The wind chimes chinked a splatter of bassy notes as Denise heaved herself and the bags onto the bow deck. *Heron's Egg* was a small boat. She was forty-five feet long with a galley, a bathroom and a single room that served as a sleeping and living area. Denise dropped the bags a little too carelessly onto the deck so she could get her keys. She winced and waited, staring at the deck, for a moment, until the lack of ooze indicated that bottles and cans remained intact. Relieved, she fitted the brass key, attached to a cork ball, into the lock. Once the door swung open Denise could smell the incense, coconut scented, she had been burning the night before. She had bought it from a stall at the market on a whim as it proclaimed it induced protection and purification. Actually, the smell only reminded Denise how long the summer, a hot, blue summer, was taking to arrive. The three steps down into the boat were the happiest steps of the day.

Denise had owned *Heron's Egg* for three years. The first two years had been tough, as the boat emptied her savings and took half her wages but the barge was now fully and totally in Denise's keeping.

She lived frugally and carefully. She had the costs of the winter mooring in the marina, the licence fee, the blacking, the gas bottle refills but was slowly she was able to rebuild her savings. As soon as the weather permitted she found a mooring on the canal where she didn't have to pay and there were no time restrictions. During the warm months she only had to spend money on the fortnightly visit to the marina for the pump out, refill of the water tank and to top up her diesel. She scavenged the canal paths for wood and so could be sparing with the coal she'd bought from the canal trader.

The downside was on one of her days off she would have to spend several hours lugging her washing to and from the laundromat in a backpack, though she tried to make it a more enjoyable activity by combining it with a catch-up with a friend. Also, she had to leave so early in the morning to get to a gym in town, where she exercised and showered. Denise had become such a regular she had led a few classes when the usual teacher failed to materialise.

Denise unloaded her shopping and held the bottle up to the light and revelled in her ability to afford some luxuries. She wished she could share a glass with a friend and for a moment felt very lonely. Her mooring out of town made it hard to meet up with friends; they were as cash-strapped as she was and only Cal owned a car. She shook her head to clear it of self-pity and went out onto the front deck but her feeling of isolation just increased. Usually there was another narrowboat or two on this stretch of the canal and it was depressing to see it so empty. Most of the other canal boats which moored outside the restriction zones were crewed by old people doing the ring. Denise sometimes felt that she was the only person on the Llangollen canal without grey hair.

Not that a nearby boat was company in any real sense but it was a reassurance.

She stepped backwards down the three stairs into her boat, stripped off her uniform, wrapped herself in her brocade dressing grown and replaced her brown shoes with fluffy slippers. Finally Denise reached up and unclipped the plait, bound for hygienic reasons to the back of her head, so that the heavy rope of black hair swung a foot below her shoulders. She pulled the binding off the end of the plait and sighed with pleasure as the tight strands unravelled and spread in a glossy fan across her shoulders and back.

She put a match to the paper, kindling and wood that was already laid in the little black stove and felt her sense of well-being soar as the fire lit readily. She poured a large glass of white wine, grabbed a cushion to soften sitting on the metal of the bow, and went outside to enjoy her drink.

Denise watched the blackbirds flirt on the towpath as she sipped her wine. Beyond them she could see pale green fields patched with sheep. The canal was raised here, a huge engineering feat achieved with picks, shovels and carts. There were ducks on the water but they ignored *Heron's Egg* as she had adamantly refused to feed them. A moor hen skittered across the water which alerted Denise to the advance of another canal boat. She could see immediately due to its livery colours that it was a hire boat and the blare of the hip hop music indicated that the crew were young and brash. She decided that being alone was to be appreciated and she hoped very, very hard that it would not moor near her.

Denise turned her body so that she had her back to the canal. She did not want any eye contact to suggest that she welcomed their presence. She thought about going inside but it was a lovely evening so she stubbornly remained in place, sipped more of the Chardonnay and counted the sheep.

The hire boat passed at too great a speed and *Heron's Egg* rocked uncomfortably and the mooring ropes whined. Denise shot a hostile glance over her shoulder and was met with whoops and whistles from the stern where three young men were draped over the roof while two others stood by the rudder. All were holding tins of cider. She felt exposed and ridiculous. The dressing gown seemed thin and her feet curled in their silly slippers. Denise sat still stiffly, keeping her back to the canal, and waited for the hire boat to move further up the canal.

It didn't.

'This looks like a good place.'

'Nice bit of scenery hereabouts.'

'Could do with stopping and getting warmed up.'

'Enough hair there to wrap around two.'

'Or three.'

The loud conversation was punctuated by guffaws of laughter and all the while the music blared. The ducks and blackbirds had decamped and even the sheep had moved up the field further away from the canal.

Denise rapidly rose to her feet and, her glass in hand, backed through the door of her boat to escape the scrutiny of the men on the passing boat. She flushed as she realised by the whistles that the gown had gaped as she bent forward. She was so flustered she banged her head, tripped off the last step off the stairs and twisted her ankle. Most of the wine from her glass spilt on the patterned rug decorating the cabin. Denise slammed the door and bolted it. The smell of coconut mocked her.

She felt very uneasy. She checked her phone but knew, even as she looked as the screen, there was no signal. If she wanted to call someone she had to walk to the bridge but now that would take her past the hire boat with its unpleasant, drunk crew. She drew a shuddering breath, and tried to quash anxiety with action. Quickly Denise walked through the boat closing the windows she had so recently opened and bolted the door. She changed into jeans, trainers and a thick jumper and tied her hair back in a ponytail. She put her pepper spray on the table and sat down to think about her options.

Staying put would involve a sleepless night and a lot of risk. Drink made people mean. Her father had been a mean man when the drink was in him which was why Denise and her mother had left. At least five yobs hammered on cider could be very nasty indeed. She could leave *Heron's Egg* and beg a stay on Helen's sofa but she feared for her boat as much as for herself. She could lie about the imminent arrival of her man and his huge dog but consequences never deterred drunks. Denise decided that she would have to shift the boat.

She looked out of the window at the hire boat and saw that they were ineptly hauling her into the side of the canal by the stern and spreading the rest of the boat across the canal. They were shouting at one another.

This was her moment. First she turned down the fire; the chimney would have to stay in place but she thought the arch of the bridge was high enough to get through. She unbolted the back of the boat and fitted the rudder with the pin. She started the engine, thankful *Heron's Egg* was a quiet boat, though the way those louts were revving their engine they wouldn't hear an aeroplane take off. Denise left the boat in neutral and, pepper spray in her pocket, walked quickly to the front of her boat, loosened the rope and unfixed the keeper which hooked into the metal shafts on the side of the canal and dropped it on the deck. Normally Denise would have neatly coiled her rope on *Heron's Egg*'s bow but these were not normal times. She pushed at the bow of her boat and it began to drift out from the bank.

The front of the hire boat had been hauled in and was being banged against the side of the canal; Denise found a moment to feel sorry for a boat in such inept hands. One of the cider swilling chaps, all of the men had a can in one hand as they pulled on the ropes or the rudder with the other, saw her. He dropped his end of the rope and rubbed his groin.

Denise felt the wine rise up sour and bitter in the back of her throat. She refused to be sick and she ran to the back of the boat and released the remaining rope that held her boat to the side of the canal. She gripped the rudder, put the engine into gear and began gliding into the centre of the canal. The contrast between her hammering heart and the slow chug of the engine was excruciating. Two men, standing on the stern of the hire boat, shouted lewd comments and signalled her to stop, as she guided *Heron's Egg*, slowly, so slowly, into the centre of the canal. For one horrible moment Denise thought one of them was going to attempt the five-foot leap from his boat to hers in response to the foul drunk on the bank shouting out, 'Grab her! Don't let her get away.'

Heron's Egg was on the far side of the canal and three yards from side of the hire boat. Denise poured on more power and *Heron's Egg* surged forward. Still shaking with fright, she put her boat into an even higher speed. When she was out of beyond the reach of the drunks she looked back and took a nasty pleasure in watching the wake toss the hire boat and her unsteady crew.

Tonight and Thursday she would stay in the marina. On the weekend she would find another mooring, one with a signal and some old bargees nearby. In future she would choose her moorings with more discretion; with an eye to safety rather than just her bank balance.

Here and There

New Blood

Lena was new to the area. She decided to join the Local Ladies Association and attended a meeting in the old red brick building in the centre of town. She made her way there and arrived fifteen minutes before the start and she sat on a chair, four rows from the front. She had scarcely placed her neat bottom on the wooden chair before she was told that was reserved. 'This, this been Annie's chair for almost twenty years!' Lena knew she should move but the impatient, clucky tone of voice made her stubborn. Lena leaned back in the chair, crossed her fifteen denier stockinged legs and made a witticism about not seeing any towels. Her comment met with a frigid silence from those in the immediate vicinity. The woman, who had told her about the reservation, grew quite red with umbrage, and began to use her wide as high bulk to bulldoze Lena off the chair.

'Actually,' Lena unwisely confided to the new neighbour ten rows behind her first selection, 'the waft of stale armpits is what really persuaded me to move.' The new neighbour, who drew back from Lena as if she herself smelt, said that she had been a member of LLA for twenty years as well and that her sympathies lay with Becky and Annie.

Lena did not stay for any more of the Local Ladies Association meeting. She clattered out, more loudly than was strictly necessary, as the members in the hall were called to order. The lipstick coated, amplified mince and pop of the Chair's pronouncements followed her through the heavy doors. Lena stood in the corridor and took stock of her situation; she and the LLA were not going to get along. She was not at all distressed by this recognition but congratulated herself on exiting such a homespun organisation earlier rather than later. Lena placed her dark brown bag and her rolled umbrella on a convenient shelf. She shook her new tan woollen coat into better order as, sliding along rows and changing chairs like she had been part of some sort of children's game, had rumpled it and she put it on over the beige slacks and thin cream alpaca sweater.

Lena tossed her head so that the pearl drop earrings comfortingly brushed her neck. She had moved away from the small city she loved after the divorce. She couldn't bear to see him prancing around with his acquisition, at least twenty years his junior; it made him look so old. She had been offered redundancy from the accountancy firm, which she had accepted graciously publicly, but it had been irksome to be replaced at work by a younger model there as well. Lena was well off but at a loose end. She had selected this particular town because it was close to Nantwich, a place she had not warmed to, where her son had set up his business.

Lena's attention was caught by the display board and she was immediately engaged by the bright, cheerful and well-dressed persons who adorned the poster advertising the existence of the CCC. 'College Community Connections', Lena savoured the words. She read the brief summary about the organization. 'A much more sympathetic group for a woman of my calibre,' Lena declared aloud. 'Nobody here I want to talk to anyway.' The door into the corridor opened and the woman who had taken her pound coins peered out. Lena collected her belongings from the shelf, turned and addressed the hovering head. 'It's all right,' she said graciously, 'I don't require my money back.' The head was hurriedly withdrawn.

Lena began to reach into her slim bag for a pen and then she simply tore the poster off the wall. She kicked the closed door with her brown court shoe, making sure it was with the sole of her shoe so the leather was not damaged, before she sauntered out.

Unwilling to be misled into attending another cardigan, dropped skirt and wooden beads affair Lena researched the College Community Connections on her iPad while having a cup of coffee, latte, in the one of several decent cafés in the town. She tapped the screen with brisk, shell-pink fingertips and was pleased with the brightness of the website declaring the variety of activities. She was wary of Facebook and Twitter, in the same way that she never bought humdrum magazines. She was adept at using Google and, although she wittily commented whenever the occasion arose that Wikipedia was just as weak as its title suggested, she was a habitual user. Lena was gratified to realise that there was a meeting of the CCC in two days' time.

On Thursday Lena combined a pale yellow shirt with beige slacks and added a patterned silk gold scarf to ensure those second looks that Lena liked to secure. The welcome at the Guild Hall venue was all that Lena could have wished: Alice, the Chair, was well dressed, well-spoken and took Lena's hand in hers when they were introduced. The talk, by an enthusiastic woman armed with a couple of hundred slides of European painters, was actually enlightening. Over tea, and no biscuits thank you I have to watch my figure, Lena joined the Gardening Club which was peopled by well-spoken, keen types. Lena was motivated by the trips the group organised to significant gardens in the locality rather than by gardening itself; she loved an outing.

When asked, Lena described her own garden as small with an emphasis on contrasts to create impact. It was a dramatic way to describe the paved back garden, borders of pebbles, a plastic bench and the single artificial cherry that had survived the blitz once she had purchased the small terraced house.

Her minimalist gardening style excused her from having to participate in the practical concerns of the club. She contributed neither vegetable nor bedding plants grown from seed. She didn't have to dig or prune, Lena liked her hands remaining scratch free, so she tuned out of those parts of the discussions. Lena did enjoy the outings. She liked the bus trips particularly because they provided an extended opportunity for the sort of intimate conversation Lena preferred. When the Gardening Club met at the home of the convener Lena would elect to sit on the couch. She thus could ask the person who sat next to her, sotto voce and leaning towards her couch-neighbour, about her health, family and recent activities while the main themes of the meeting swirled predictably around them.

Lena also joined the Painting Class. Lena liked to use watercolour. She was a veteran of several art courses, a hobby she had pursued when she lived in the city, and she revelled in being able to pass on the knowledge that she had acquired. Indeed, she spent considerably more time critiquing other painters' work than she did painting her own still life scenes. Still, it was universally accepted that she did know what she was talking about and Mr Green's use of perspective had significantly improved under her tutelage before he stopped attending.

Within six months Lena was on the committee of the CCC. Alice had announced that there was a vacancy and Lena was more than willing to take up a role that so many inexplicably eschewed. Lena was delighted when she was appointed, the election was uncontested. She liked meetings, she liked having access to the membership lists, she liked being a guiding hand, she liked the gravitas and structure being a committee member gave to her diary.

Lena relished her first outing as a committee member. She dressed carefully in a pale floral dress with cornflower blue bolero, blue sandals and a dash of Dewberry. When the meeting was brought to order Lena rummaged in her capacious white beach bag and took out a notebook and pen. The secretary informed Lena, twice, that she would be sent copies of the minutes, but Lena persisted in making her own record of the discussion onto to paper in a looping longhand. She was always grateful for those people who insisted on saying the same dull thing several times as it gave her the opportunity to record the more colourful comments she knew, from past experience, that a secretary always left out of a report. At one point she had a bit of time for extensive doodling during the computer stuff, she had unsuccessfully tried to engaged committee member Catherine in an exchange of whispers, until the Chair moved on to another matter on the agenda.

She loitered after the others had left, despite being told by the secretary, who was also a member of Lena's painting group, about Alice being due to meet her daughter in the afternoon. Alice hesitated but, resigned to entertaining her guest for a bit longer, asked Lena if she would like anther cup of tea. 'It is always nice to have tea for two.' She and Alice laughed at her little joke. Lena liked Alice. She was a popular woman and being with her provided an entrée into the bigger picture. Alice, Lena had elicited, was a divorced woman too and she had recently retired from her position as receptionist at a primary school. She had lived in the area for quite a long time which was also an advantage because she would be able to provide Lena with an in-depth understanding. 'You,' Lena confided to Alice, 'have done well to live all this time here without falling prey to the dreadful dreary and drab fashions that epitomised the LLA.'

Alice gulped her tea and fidgeted while Lena sipped slowly at her own as she asked for more particulars about character of the Treasurer. Lena shared her plan to assume the role in good time. 'I really don't mean to hurry you, Lena,' Alice finally said after another five minutes had passed, 'but I must get on with getting ready for Pamela's arrival.'

'Your lovely, lovely daughter!' said Lena. 'I have enjoyed seeing her pictures here in the house after I have heard so much about her. Oh, I do look forward to meeting her.' Lena stood, gathered up the bag containing the notebook, and moved in the direction of the door shepherded by Alice. At the door Lena turned and took Alice's tanned hand in her own red- nailed, white fingers 'I am so glad we will see each other often.' Her minty breath caressed Alice's cheek.

The Shout

Eddie, Roland's father had liked to have his family around him. He liked to have them, the family, supping at his table and sucking up his words of wisdom. He kept tabs on his large family throughout the year through invitation and inquisition but he also liked to gather them together under one roof on the third weekend every six months. Non-attendance was not an option, not that Roland, second son, would have even considered ever missing one. Though the gatherings always made Roland more belligerent, Luka had learnt it was futile to try and persuade him not to go.

When Eddie died the family sold the huge family home after they had shifted their drained mother into a care facility. Mari, the eldest, had hosted the bi-annual event once in her house and refused to do so again. 'I'm not putting up with it. They expect to be waited on hand and foot while they drink and boast and swear,' she'd announced to her husband, Ray. 'I'm no lackey for their convenience! We've got out interests to look after as well.'

Luka had hoped the family function would die as well. However, the family moved their meeting place to a nearby pub; they continued to meet three times a year. It was more because their business interests in vans, house clearances and removals meshed than in affection. Some cousins, who were so distant that they fell into the colleague category and would have never made it over the threshold when Eddie was alive, came along to try and get a toe in some of the deals.

Roland never missed one of these meetings. He, and therefore Luka and Leon, stayed in the pub as well as ate and drank in it. Without the strictures of a home environment the number of family members attending had grown in proportion to a slump in manners. This was the second day and the mood was, as usual, generally nastier. The dinner, the same old rowdy affair, had been over for a couple of hours. Roland was busy talking deals with several cousins.

Luka stopped Jan reaching for her purse with a gentle touch. 'My shout,' she told Jan, who looked surprised. Luka went to the bar and signalled to the bartender. Jan, a loud, kind woman, provided a welcome refugee from the hustle and edge which characterised the rest of Roland's family. Luka handed over a crumpled five pound note for the two pints placed on the bar towel.

Suddenly Ray muscled in next to her and swept them away. 'Buying drinks? I'll have a pint and so will Sam.' Luka stared at him in dismay as he took a swig of one beer and passed the other to his right into waiting hands of his yob of a son.

She waved her key at the bartender but he refused to let her begin a tab so she could purchase another couple of pints. She knew, as her stomach churned with anxiety and indecision, that no matter how long she fumbled in her handbag there was no money as she had been on that hunt yesterday.

'Keeps you short, does he?' Ray sneered over the pint glass through the froth on his lip. 'Mean bastard! Well, you'll just have to trot over and get good old Rolly to cough up some more lolly. He owes me a couple of drinks.' Luka pressed her trembling lips together. 'He left me in the lurch so don't come the misery guts with me because I'm not going to put my hand in my pocket.'

'Just a moment,' she gasped to no-one as Ray and the bartender had already turned away from her. She looked towards Jan and made a scrambled signal with her hand and then she took a breath and headed for the table where Roland was holding forth.

'I need a bit more money for drinks,' she gabbled, interrupting her husband. Roland stiffened. He looked past her to the bar where Ray, his smart-arse brother-in-law, was propped; he was holding a pint up and giving him a cheesy grin. 'Please,' Luka begged, 'I have to buy Jan a drink. I promised her I would get this round. She has bought me a couple of drinks already.'

'No,' he said. He was flushed with anger and beer. 'No. No more money.'

'But please,' said Luka, 'I have to.' Her words stuttered to a halt because Roland had gripped her wrist and he was squeezing as he pulled her onto the chair beside him. He squeezed even harder and Luka bent forward over her arm with the pain.

'No, you don't. No, you won't.' He released her and chuckled at his own wit. 'Now, don't ask me again, Loopy, there's a good girl.' He patted the bruised arm. 'It'll do Jan good to go without; all that beer is making her fat.' He turned his back on his wife and resumed his loud conversation with his cousins, all of whom had watched the little drama between Rolly and Luka as if it were on television.

Luka felt marooned. She wondered if she was going to be sick and fixed her eyes on the sodden beer mat. She didn't dare look in Jan's direction. She knew Ray and Sam would have watched the whole performance and enjoyed their success in getting a rise out of Rolly. As soon as she believed it would be permitted she lurched to her feet. She paused when Roland turned to look at her. 'Off you hop now,' he gave her the all clear to leave.

Luka weaved her way out of the bar without making eye contact with anyone. She nursed her bruised wrist in one pocket and her fingers were wrapped around the key to the room in the other. The small apartment offered some level of sanctuary but not much because she knew that Leon was there. Coping with her bruises would have been so much easier at home where she could have retreated childishly to the world of beds and blankets or the end of the garden.

Leon was spread-eagled across the brown sofa bed with both hands on the joystick that connected him to the large television screen. He didn't answer when Luka spoke to him. She went into the bedroom, hung her checked jacket on the back of a chair and gathered together some casual clothes and went into the bathroom.

Luka sat on the lid of the toilet while she ran cold water over her red wrist. She stared at herself in the mirror; heavy eye make-up and dark red lipstick glared out of a sallow face. She still felt sick and she could see that her dress was blotched with wet patches under the arms.

Luka almost jerked off the seat by the hammering on the door. 'Hey, Loopy,' shouted Leon. He had taken to using the insulting name that Roland had recently dubbed her with instead of Mum. 'I want some food. I want you to go to a shop and get it for me,' Leon said these words using the same hectoring inflections as his father.

Suddenly Luka felt as if she were on fire with anger. She stripped off her fancy dress and dragged on jeans, jumper and boots.

Leon had resumed his position on the sofa. He looked at his mother with disdain. 'I called Dad and he said there's some money in his wallet in the drawer of the bedside table and to tell you to take a tenner and go and get me some food. And you'd better be damned quick about it!' Leon turned towards the television and Luca's answer died in her throat. The familiar heat of her resentment vanished; instead she turned cold and felt a tremendous distance yawn between herself and Rolly's lout of a son. 'Go on. Hop to it.' The distance grew bigger and colder.

Luka went into the bedroom. The wallet, Luka saw, contained three hundred pounds and a couple of credit cards. She put wallet and car keys into her handbag, hitched it over her shoulder, and walked carefully into the main room.

Leon flicked his fingers at her, the same gesture his father used to indicate dismissal. Luka felt as if she was watching him from the moon. She dropped the key to the room on to the sofa beside the boy and said, 'It's late. It'll take me time to find the right sort of place. I may be gone a while.'

Changing Tunes

The house was cheap. Very cheap! It was obvious why with the electricity pylons squatting nearby but I wanted my own house, and to have one in the country was the icing on the cake. 'I don't have to look at them,' I told myself firmly,

Mrs Wilson, two years widowed, was desperate to sell and move back to her home town in Lancashire. I couldn't believe my luck finding a house in good condition, with half an acre of garden and a comfortable drive to work. I made an offer within hours of seeing the house. Mrs Wilson, via her agency, accepted immediately. I wasn't completely brainless and kept my joy buttoned down until the various conveyancing checks came back clean. The legalities and payments were to be settled by the end of July.

We exchanged contracts even though I had only visited the house once. I had asked Mrs Wilson if I could call in before she moved out but she was evasive. 'It's all in the floor plan,' she said the first time. 'Sorry. It's not convenient today as I've stuff all over the floor sorting for the move,' she said on the second occasion and the third.

I longed to have another look at my soon-to-be home. I had lurked in the lane in my car a few times looking at the Holly Cottage from a distance. I had driven a friend to the end of the drive to admire the house though we could only see the gable windows and the roof.

'One of those pylons is awfully close,' said Ann as we drove towards the A5.

'The main reason I could afford the house,' I had replied carelessly. 'I was more put off by stink of her cigarette smoke, to be honest.'

Here and There

I contacted Mrs Wilson again, a couple of weeks before the agreed moving date; she responded reluctantly to my impatience and frustration by agreeing to let me revisit the house. I may have mentioned that I was prepared to pull out even if it would cost me my deposit.

The three-hundred-yard drive to Holly Cottage was overhung with grasses. Through the patchy foliage of the unkempt hedge, some of which was indeed holly, I could see the large garden, at the front of the house, was even more neglected. I shivered with pleasure; I would create the garden I wanted.

I parked outside the garage which was solid though the paint was peeling. Mrs Wilson, cream blouse and dark tweed skirt, dashed out as soon as I opened the car door and urged me into the cottage through the back door. I was reluctant as I wanted to look around the half an acre of land but, as I felt a bit guilty about the method I'd used to coerce her, I consented to be ushered into the kitchen. I would look around the garden on my way out.

The smell of cigarettes was less pungent. The kitchen, stripped of utensils, looked more tired that I remembered. I knew Mrs Wilson had lived in Holly Cottage for at least ten years but the fittings were considerable older than that. I was surprised all over again that they had not updated when they had moved in. Well, they would have to last a while longer as I didn't have much money left to do anything after the purchase. The radio was blaring, as it had been on my first visit to the house, but I asked her to turn it down this time. She did so grudgingly and she must have bumped the tuning when she twisted the volume dial because there was bleed of static through the music.

Over a cup of tea she told me, 'I'm going back to Bury. I've enough to buy a terrace near my sister.'

I was surprised and a bit worried that she might want to delay completion. 'I thought you had a property lined up to go to. I am committed to moving in the last weekend of the month.'

Mrs Wilson's face flickered and her hands stopped fussing with her tea cup. 'You've organised the removal van then?' she asked and when I nodded she sighed with pleasure. 'You've given your notice to the landlord!' This time she was not asking a question but I nodded again anyway. Mrs Wilson beamed at me. This was the first time I had seen her smile. I felt pretty bad about making her believe that I would really pull out of the sale at such a late stage.

'It's all in the pipeline,' I assured her. 'I just wanted to get a better of idea of the cottage so I can direct the removal men when they get here.'

'And I have every intention of moving out on our agreed date,' she told me. The soft skin pouched around her pursed mouth. The smile was gone. 'I am able to stay with my sister until something suitable turns up. She is alone too.'

'Bit of a change from this rural scene,' I commented.

'I won't be sorry to leave,' she replied with venom. 'These bloody green fields and hedgerows haven't been much of a comfort.' I must have looked shocked because she pressed her lips more tightly together and stood up. She rushed me through a tour of the two-bedroom cottage. She slept in the smaller bedroom. I presumed the large one, which was dark and airless, had lost its appeal after her husband died. She confirmed that she would be leaving the fittings, curtains, fridge and washing machine as we had agreed. I was pleased with the size of the sitting room, though I had to look at it with the electric light on because the thick heavy curtains were closely drawn.

When I asked to look around the garden Mrs Wilson said that she was going out and I would have to wait until I moved in and took possession. We arranged that I would come to the cottage at 10am and she would hand over the keys and I could organise the delivery of my goods to suit me after that.

By the time the day to move arrived I was fizzing with joy. I had decided I would take possession all on my own. I packed an airbed and some toiletries and arrived at Holly Cottage a few minutes early. Mrs Wilson was sitting in her car inside the garage. As she got out of the car I could hear chatter from her car radio. She waved at me to park my car to the right of the garage on a square of cement. 'I moved out last week,' she said. She handed me the keys immediately and she smiled, showing all of her teeth.

I was trembling; I was so excited. My own home! This neat cottage with a large garden was so much more than I had ever thought I would be able to afford. It was so wonderfully different from the bland, cloned house I had rented in a dull suburban backwater for several years. I looked at the keys in my hand and giggled.

'The door is unlocked,' Mrs Wilson said and we went into the kitchen. I couldn't help myself and I twirled around on my toes. 'Well, I hope you will be happier here than I was, Miss Smith.' Mrs Wilson had stopped smiling. Now that she was no longer anxious I realised that the main emotion her face conveyed was sourness.

'Why shouldn't I be happy?' I tossed the keys in the air and caught them. 'Is there a ghost?'

Mrs Wilson laughed. She laughed until she had to lean against the kitchen bench. 'A ghost!' she gurgled. 'A ghost!' She stopped laughing as dramatically as she had started. She tugged her pale blue shirt into place over her navy slacks and patted strands of hair off her flushed face. 'I wish it had been a ghost instead of those monstrosities.' I was repulsed by her hysterics and I stepped away from her. She in turn looked offended.

Suddenly she smiled with stretched lips and displayed her smoker's dark edged teeth. 'Come with me, Miss Smith,' she said in her practised clerk's voice. She led the way into the lounge room and stood by the by the windows for a moment. She pushed the curtains apart so impatiently one sagged off the rail. A huge electricity pylon stood barely fifteen yards from the window.

I must admit I was surprised by just how close the pylon was to the house.

It had been marked on the plans. I had been aware that it was part of a team marching across Bagley Marsh but on my earlier visits I had entered from the opposite side and the buildings and the fruit trees had disguised its proximity. I'd even blessed it as I'd only been able to afford the cottage because of that pylon.

Now, the pylon loomed liked a skeletal Titan and the wires and transformers stretched out like tortured muscles. Not a great view but even so, I was puzzled about why Mrs Wilson pointed at the steel construction as if it was a demon.

'Can't you hear it?' she hissed. I shook my head. I wished that she would get on and leave. She opened the SUV windows, triple glazed, according to the survey. 'Listen,' she commanded and so I did.

A high, continuous buzz surrounded me. It wasn't very loud but, now that I was aware of the sound, it seemed to fill my head with bees. I backed away from the window and turned to see Mrs Wilson looking at me with nasty satisfaction. 'It's such a dreadful, dreadful noise! It buzzes like a dentist's drill on damp days.' As she spoke I began to think that I could feel the prickly hum of the electricity pylon as an actual tremor in the house. I realised that my knees were shaking and I propped myself against the wall by the sitting room door.

I thought I'd go mad some days!' She rubbed her upper arms with her hands. 'Alan wouldn't leave, no matter how much I pleaded. He told me I was just fidgeting about a bit of noise and to stop listening to it.' Mrs Wilson's hands wrapped themselves tightly about her elbows. 'It has a deadly tone to it, I'd tell him. It makes my teeth ache, I'd say to him. I can't sleep, I would tell him night after night. He put in the windows and then he ignored me, spent all his time in garden. And we stayed.'

I stared at her. The high pitched drone from the pylon was making me itch.

'But now I can go.' She looked relieved and tired. 'Not just into town. Or get away by insisting to Alan that we went on a holiday.' She straightened and smiled at me. 'Now, I can go forever. I never, ever have to come back here.'

She walked out of the sitting room briskly and I followed her, minus the jig in my step or heart. I felt as if the sound of the wires was stalking me through the house. Mrs Wilson picked up her bag from the kitchen bench and looked at her watch. 'I have left you some milk in the fridge and a few teabags. My new address is written here and I would appreciate it if you would redirect my mail though I am sure that I have done as much as I can to alert them to my new address. Well, my dear, I wish you well in your new home.' She smiled in a mean way, this time without showing her teeth. I disliked her intensely. The pleasure I had in my new home was spluttering and I had barely been in the cottage thirty minutes.

I was summoning the reserves to wish her well in return when she turned, having stepped through the kitchen door onto the path, and she spoke again. 'Well, I won't miss this dreadful constant sawing sound.' She paused and we both listened to the insistent faint ominous buzz of the high tension electricity wires. I felt my heart flutter with horror as I realised she was leaving me alone with her monstrosities. Then I realised Mrs Wilson was enjoying my misery so I said nothing and slammed the door. I stood behind it and waited until I heard her car drive away.

For a while I stood leaning against the door, full of grief. The buzz seemed to be getting louder. Would I end up like bitter Mrs Wilson?

I rushed into the sitting room where the hissing buzz of the electricity wires surged through the open window. I felt overpowered and depressed by the noise. This was just like the time at school when Jack, who sat next to me in Biology, had asked me whether I could hear the fluorescent light tubes. Once he had alerted me to the mosquito-like sound it pursued me and irritated me for rest of the year.

I slammed the window shut and went into the kitchen where the sound was more muted. I wondered if the dog I always wanted would be able to cope with the noise. I could see the pitying looks from my friends and family. The words 'disaster' and 'idiot' buzzed in my head as constantly as the noise from the wires.

I had to get out of the house. I was about to dash down the drive away from the pylons but halted and turned into the garden. The noise on the side of the house, closest to the pylon, was a strident fizz. I was astonished that I had been so unaware of it during my two visits. I felt tears prick at my eyes and shook my head savagely to drive them away.

The sun was shining strongly. The white walls of Holly Cottage gleamed. The pylon sketched shadows across the garden; hatched like the ancient cave paintings. The buzz was a permanent mosquito in my ears. Before, I had considered pylons as elegant Eiffel structures reaching their arms out to dance, now, the looming pylon was a massive, ugly piece of Meccano with its struts sunk into a barren slab of concrete.

I headed diagonally across the garden over weedy grass to the stile I knew from the site maps gave me access to the footpath. It went across a couple of fields to the Montgomery Canal. The pylons marched beside me across the field as well. I could hear them hissing at me. As I walked I slashed at the vegetation with a scrap of a stick.

When I reached the canal I turned south away from the pylons and out of reach of their insidious noise. I kept going until I reached the lock and slumped onto the wooden seat there. If I looked north I could still see the pylons dominating the landscape with steel arms akimbo.

I focussed fiercely on the canal. A narrow boat had recently passed through and the lock was empty but I could hear the constant splash of water through leaking gates. I reckoned the lock would refill in an hour. On the other side of the hump-backed bridge was Lock Cottage. It boasted a lot more rooms and glass than when it had been first been built and the owners obviously liked roses. I wondered what they thought of the periodic noise of the boats and walkers but I imagined they would be soothed by the constant sound of the slosh of water.

I bounded off the seat. 'The key,' I said the words aloud and laughed at my own pun. 'The key,' I almost sang the words as I stared at wonderful Lock Cottage, 'is not to get in a knot.' I laughed again.

I was suffused with a steely determination to take possession of Holly Cottage in spite of the pylons. I would be a Mr Wilson, 'just a bit of noise', rather than like that bitch, Mrs Wilson, who had tried to pass me the baton of her miserable, negative attitude. The joy I felt in owning Holly Cottage rushed in like a turning tide. I tossed the stick into the hedge as I strode along the towpath. A small breeze had picked up and I could hear the susurration of the common reed.

I would plant reeds and other noisy plants in the garden. I could hang wind chimes. I could have a water feature. It would block or complement the sound of the pylon.

I picked up my pace. I just wanted to get home. I wanted to get home to Holly Cottage.

Staying Put

Things weren't going to plan!

Marcus was away for several days; called away for a training programme he thought he'd been able to wriggle out of. He was required to attend so 'they' could tell him what he already knew by presenters who rebranded effective routines with new headings. Angela had a weekend arrangement and Jack was on a bus to France for a skiing holiday.

So Rosa was left at home alone. She had been very jolly about it all during the hugs, kisses and waves. She agreed she would be all right though she did note that all of her family said these words to her as a statement rather than as a question. Indeed Rosa didn't mind being in the house by herself. She had the hens to see to, wild birds to feed and the dogs to walk; she was sure that dogs constituted companionship. Moreover she loved her home; it was familiar, comfortable and attractive, and she was proud of the work she and Marcus had put into making it so.

Still, as Angela's car turned onto the road with a cheeky tootle of the horn, Rosa felt abandoned. She felt, as she had always felt when waving goodbye from station platforms, bus terminals and airport lounges, the ones on the move were going to have a much better time than the one left behind. Despite her determinedly cheery façade she could not stop words like isolated, deserted and forsaken bubbling through her mind with a particular intensity, almost a horror.

The solution to such situations Rose knew was to be busy. She threw herself into imposing order on the debris left by her family. She raced through the routine chores much more quickly than if she had had to negotiate their performance with someone else. By ten in the morning Rosa had pushed a second load into the dryer, washed and put away the dishes, emptied bins and swept through the kitchen with a broom. When she stopped for a coffee she told the dogs, smooching for biscuit crumbs, that she was still feeling a bit hollowed out.

'Hollow! Hollow! Full of holes. Holey and wholly unwanted!' she expounded further on her feeling of neglect. Rosa was shocked by the intensity with which she uttered these words. It would be all too easy to denigrate herself; belittle herself into a ragged, humdrum drudge. She was suddenly aware she was only a short slide from a full-blown case of self-pity and misery.

Rosa raced over to the hi-fi and the looping, waterfall music and lyrics of the Moulettes began; good start in helping to keep the blues at bay even if the third song was about a stalker.

The problem with a sense of abandonment is it cultivates feelings of worthlessness and those play havoc with attempts to get motivated. Rosa turned the music up a couple of notches but still dithered about what to do next. She liked to read and she had work to do on her laptop but her feet itched; she knew she was too unsettled to sit down. She thought about going to town but the cold east wind made the prospect of waiting for a bus very unattractive; Marcus had taken the car to Durham so any idea of a bigger trip was out of the question. She should exercise but she'd already walked the dogs and, although the music was cheering, she couldn't persuade herself to dance to it, this time.

That left the other method Rosa used to thrust the doldrums away which was to makes physical changes to her environment.

Rosa hauled the vacuum cleaner out of the cupboard and lugged it into the lounge. Her dyed in the wool solution to emptiness was cleanliness. 'Next to godliness,' she informed the dogs, cowering on their beds, because neither liked the sound or the jerking movements made by the sucking machine. Actually it wasn't in fact the cleaning Rosa was interested in but the permission it gave her to move furniture and change the look of the room. She found rearranging the pictures, shifting chairs and side tables to new sites, repositioning the pieces of glass and wood and trying a new angle with the rugs satisfying and relaxing.

Marcus hated it! 'What's been changed?' he would sigh. He seemed to know before he stepped over the threshold when Rosa had been 'at it again'. He was of the same state of mind as his mother who had not moved the position of any of her furniture for fifty years. 'I like to know where things are!' he would complain. They had had a particularly vigorous disagreement about 'moving stuff' when he had fallen over a repositioned bench in the garden on his way to close up the chooks after dark.

Rosa had admitted it was a bit odd but not very. 'Everyone has ways of making peace with their world,' she consoled her husband. 'It could be worse! Sandra puts stencils in her bathrooms; they are beginning to look like a man with too many unrelated tattoos.' Marcus had been unimpressed. 'Jill plays heavy metal music at maximum volume while she dusts! The neighbours tolerate it because they know it won't last the hour. Carla bakes muffins most of which end up on the bird table. John makes weirdly spiced jams or sorbets out of fruit he had frozen during a glut. You,' Rosa had waggled her finger at her husband, 'play in your potato patch or go cycling.'

'But why move the bed from its sensible position in the centre of the room to this weird angle? Why?'

'You can see into the garden more easily,' Rosa had responded. 'I've put the binoculars there so we can bird watch. You like birdwatching.'

It had taken Rosa a long time to understand she moved objects within her house when she was feeling stuck. Stuck in the mud! Stuck with this little life! Stuck here and not buzzing off and doing interesting things. She was not searching out new horizons or seeking exciting opportunities. She was not being exposed to the challenge of strange, new people. She was not making waves and influencing things. She was stuck in this house, on this street, connected by well-known routes to work and time-tabled play, and she was not moving. Rosa switched off the vacuum cleaner which was brushing a section of the floor where the chair used to be and remembered what it was like to move.

Her father and mother had casually uprooted their family numerous times. Rosa, the eldest, had attended fourteen different schools though she thought the number of houses was slightly less.

Rosa recalled how resentful she had been each time she was uprooted; wrenched out like a tooth.

She had been powerless to prevent any move her parents initiated. Her objections were ignored and she was swept up and taken away: away from carefully crafted arrangements in her bedroom; away from newly-made, iridescent friendships; and away from the hard won knowledge of the place. Always she had been desperately sad to realise the habitat in which she had been fighting to get a toehold would hardly miss her.

Every time her dependence and her minority meant she had to acquiesce to another relocation Rosa had vowed she would, when she could, make herself a steady, entrenched life; she had sworn she would build a life where she would see the seasons and generations from a single vantage point.

And she'd got it, in spades.

Rosa looked around the altered room and sat down in the chair, now closer to the window, from where she could see the large established garden. She could see the huge trees she had first know as saplings. She and Marcus had buried two beloved dogs in the orchard where the apples trees she had planted were promising a good crop. She felt the bubble of discontent pop. The music was simply joyous and no longer a life belt.

She walked to the kitchen and put on the kettle. She looked at her mobile phone and saw the message from Marcus to say he had arrived in Durham. She adored this home they had made together. From here their children went to local schools, only two schools, where they had followed the curriculum from bottom to top and worked their way up the ladder in local competitions. They had friends they had known for hundreds of years. She knew her neighbours and she was long-standing member of a couple of local groups.

But, but, but. Rosa knew that moving had also been thrilling. The horizon always promised another opportunity to make it better, to be fresh and to be reinvented. She knew there was relief in being able to shake off the debris of the old place; not all of her efforts to 'fit in' had been successful or clever. She had been able to leave and ignore the gaping holes in her scholastic understanding; just leave and avoid doing anything substantial about it. And the place between, when the family had been in transit, had been peculiarly joyous. For a while she didn't have to try because, along with the rest of the family in the car on the road to the next place, they were sure of rainbows and greener pastures around the corner.

It was that mirage of promises, which urged her to forsake the settled life and move on, she quashed by heaving furniture. The sense of claustrophobia, engendered by 'these same old walls', she answered by moving a picture to another position. She quelled the desire for the minimalist life, derived from living out of a suitcase, by repositioning an item with a long and loving story.

Rosa felt settled and happy. This home existed because she had chosen, and now chose again, to stay in this place with people she loved.

When the telephone rang Rosa was buoyant. 'Yes, Marcus, I am fine, fine. I'm not at all upset. Don't worry there's not too much change this time. Yes, I promise I won't touch your shed. Anyway, I am going out with Jenny. She's picking me up. Looks like I won't have the time to muck things about too much.'

W Lodwick Lowdon

W. Lodwick Lowdon was born in Melbourne. Her pioneering ancestors made the long, dangerous voyage to Australia by ship in the 1850s looking for gold, in the 1860's looking for land, in 1911 looking for a better life for their children and in 1921 one brave young woman immigrated on her own. Her father and mother waltzed four children around the Eastern States of Australia and then moved their abode to Singapore, to Los Angeles and also to Jakarta. Education was garnered on the hop but it was valued: they packed books then stuffed clothes in around the edges, they wrote diaries and letters, they were members of libraries, read papers cover to cover, argued the toss and visited places of cultural significance.

Travelling and looking for better opportunities is in the blood.

Once she was in command of her own life W. Lodwick Lowdon worked as a waitress, for a publishing company, as a History and English teacher, as a carer, in a Scuba Dive Shop and for Amnesty International in the Eastern States of Australia. She married a Scot, has lived in England for thirty years, worked as an English teacher, built a family, made a host of friends, wrote stories and rescued kelpies.

Whenever possible the family Lowdon have always travelled!

Also available from Leaf by Leaf Press.

A Perfect Alibi
R J Turner

Richard Downs, an ageing, mid-list crime writer, suffers a severe stroke and dies in hospital, with his daughter at his bedside.
She arranges his funeral, but when his coffin is about to be lowered into the grave a terrible discovery is made. During the investigation that follows, Jane begins to learn some horrid truths about her father.

'A thoroughly gripping tale from a writer who deserves a wider audience.'
Dave Andrews, author of 'The Oswestry Round' and the Himalayan journal 'Gobowen to Everest'.

Purchase from www.leafbyleafpress.com

Also available from Leaf by Leaf Press.

It's Not A Boy!
Vicky Turrell

"It's not a boy!" shouted Posty as he carried the sad news round the scattered houses in the little village of Gum. He was used to bringing bad news in the war and saw no reason to stop.

A girl had been born to a farming family who really wanted a boy. This is the voice of that little girl, now eleven years old, telling her story.

Brought up on a remote farm in Yorkshire in the 1940s and '50s, she shows how her birth was a bombshell to her farming parents.

Living in rural isolation, she saw and interpreted, in her own inexperienced way, all aspects of human life.

To make up for not being a boy she devised a list of things she was good at so that she could succeed and make her parents proud of her. But is her list good enough?

This story was inspired by real events although some scenes and people have been invented for the purpose of the narrative. The language used is of its time.

Purchase from www.leafbyleafpress.com

Also available from Leaf by Leaf Press.

In Free Fall
B. Pearson

This collection of poems spans forty years, one marriage, two children several breakdowns, and a treasury of friendships. It is I hope accessible, diverting at times comforting and constructively disconcerting. The poems tell of someone trying to make out whether that is the sky or the ground beneath him.

"*In Free Fall* gives us Bernard Pearson's distinctive and charming voice at its emotive best. With his command of form, wit and individual sense of music, the poet celebrates people, place and nature, offering us powerful reminiscence, unforgettable endings and lyrical grace."
Jonathon Edwards. Winner Costa Book Award for Poetry 2014

Purchase from www.leafbyleafpress.com